A Handyman for the Holidays

VALERIE GOMEZ

*To anyone who's ever felt like they aren't being heard.
I hear you.*

And for my Grampo Frank, the original quiet one.

Print ISBN: 979-8-9884748-5-2

Peter Senftleben: editor
Jackson Hollingsworth: line editor/sensitivity reader

Thank you for taking the time to read *A Handyman for the Holidays*. My intention with this book was to create a feel-good romance while uplifting and giving a voice to someone who can't speak. I've tried my best to do the appropriate research and to treat my main character's disability with care and sensitivity.

Content warnings: Verbal apraxia, deaf child, social anxiety, ableism toward a nonspeaker, ableism in the form of audism, internalized ableism, mild swearing, heavy kissing, mild alcohol consumption, and a child becoming temporarily lost in a crowded place. Brief mentions of: cancer and medical trauma, economic hardship and medical bills, and IVF treatment and pregnancy.

A Handyman for the Holidays is a small-town MM romance novella published as part of Home for the Holidays, a collection of standalone novellas connected by a singular theme: spreading queer joy during the holiday season.

CHAPTER 1

FRANK

"Hey, Frank, it's Marybeth. My dryer's been making a loud squeaking sound every time I use it. Do you think you could come by and look at it sometime this week? I'm hoping to have it fixed before Thanksgiving. Text me and let me know, thanks!"

"Frank. David here. That storm that blew through a couple days ago knocked a tree limb onto the roof and my wife won't let me up on a ladder to take care of it. She says I'm too old and I'll break my neck. Too old, my ass! I'm not, and I won't. But I won't hear the end of it if I do it myself. Would you mind getting it for me? I'll send you home with some of her chocolate chip cookies for your troubles. Thanks."

"Frankie dear, it's Evelyn. I just stuck my cane through a loose board on my porch and nearly fell and broke my hip—the good one! Could you be a sweetheart and come to the house when you have a moment and fix it for me? I'll make you lunch. Bye, sweetheart."

Tapping my pen on the table, I listen to each voicemail and jot down requests and notes. I text those who have cell phones to confirm I've gotten their messages. Some elderly folks in town still use landlines, so I don't bother replying to them. They already know they can count on me.

Opening the back door to the deck of my modest, cabin-style home, I inhale lungfuls of crisp, fall air. My two dogs bolt outside and I watch as they wander into the woods surrounding the house. The cold breeze carries scents of early morning frost, woodsmoke from the fireplace, and the sweet smell of dry sycamore leaves.

Northern Michigan is magical this time of year—the months between Halloween and New Year's, when college football season is winding down and the holiday season is ramping up. There's a palpable excitement in the air for the people of Cherry Tree, either because of football playoffs, the holidays, or simply that the coffee shop in town is selling pumpkin spice in every form imaginable. Once January comes, folks hunker down for a long, cold winter. But right now, everything is perfect.

I fill my travel mug with coffee and whistle for the dogs to come inside. Shrugging on the faded black Carhartt coat that once belonged to my father, I try not to let the memories of him chopping wood, singing "Feliz Navidad" (one of the ~~most annoying~~ greatest Christmas songs ever made), and hauling out blankets with giant prints of tigers and horses—a staple in any Mexican household—overwhelm me with nostalgia.

My dad, Francisco Garza Sr., was my idol, my world. When I was a kid, I hated my name, especially when older folks would pinch my cheeks and call me "Little Frankie." I always thought the name made me sound like an old man. I wanted something *cool* like Gavin or Luke. But now that my dad is gone and I'm nearly forty, I'm proud to share a name with him.

Since moving back to town halfway through my sophomore year of college eighteen years ago, I've followed in my dad's footsteps as a woodworker and general fixer. Living in the middle of a heavily forested area in northern Michigan—and a thirty-minute drive to the next largest city—people here have learned to rely on each other for help. They always knew they could count on my dad. And now, they count on me.

I pull a red beanie, hand-knit by Evelyn, over my hair and tug on my sturdy work boots. I scratch each dog behind the ears, then shut the door behind me, leaving them to laze around in the warmth of the house. After placing a few tools in the back of my truck, I slide into the driver's seat and head to town.

While being the local on-call handyman isn't my job, not really, I feel I owe the people of Cherry Tree so much. They helped me and my family a lot when I was a kid, and I'm happy to continue to repay their kindness. Plus, doing good deeds around town not only keeps me from being lonely, but I never run out of free food or desserts that I'm given as a thank you.

I'm kneeling on Evelyn's front porch inspecting the loose board that gave her trouble this morning, while she stands just inside the screen door sipping tea and chatting away. As I work, I pick up tidbits here and there: "Little Maisy Hale lost a tooth," and "Michael caught his nanny looking through his wife's dresser while the baby was asleep," and "My new neighbor and his daughter just moved here from New York," and on and on.

Evelyn's as sweet as the butterscotch candies she keeps on her kitchen table, and I love her, I really do. But she lives alone and loves sharing gossip, despite my disinterest in the various affairs, pregnancies, disputes, or dramas of others. She knows I can't speak, and that I don't like to use my phone to type responses while I'm working. Still, she keeps up the one-sided conversation. I suspect this is her way of being social. Or perhaps, like my handyman work, this is her way of staving off loneliness.

When I'm done, Evelyn disappears back into her house while I put my tools away. She emerges a minute later with a sandwich sealed in a plastic bag and a slice of chocolate cake on a paper plate.

"I'm sorry, Frankie," she says, handing me the food. "I don't have any Tupperware for the cake. You'll have to eat it now, or drive carefully so it doesn't fall over."

I smile and nod my thanks to her.

"Thank you, sweetie," she calls from the porch as I close the door to my truck. I give her a little wave, then back out of the driveway.

Today, I manage to get all my requests taken care of by midmorning, so I head home. I'm eager to get back to the quiet comfort of my house just outside of town, surrounded by tall trees and stillness. It's not that I dislike company; I like helping my neighbors. Yet somehow, I always feel drained when I spend a lot of time with people I don't know well, people who don't know me well—which is everybody.

Bumping along the dirt road that leads to my driveway, the towering pines gradually part to reveal a charming A-frame that fits the setting perfectly, as if the house has been here as long as the forest itself. I own a swath of land that borders a lake on one side, with the house nestled just a few hundred feet from the rocky shore.

As I climb the wooden steps to the front porch that stretches across the entire width of the house, I make a mental note to sweep away fallen leaves and pinecones this afternoon. Behind the door, the dogs let out excited yips and barks, and I instantly feel lighter. Coming home to the wagging tongues, snuffles of wet noses, and the thumping of tails on the doorframe always comforts me.

Butter—the blue heeler with one blue eye and one brown eye that I'd found as a puppy, abandoned by the highway—is always the first one outside. She shoves her nose, then her head and body through the barely open door. She vibrates with excitement, jumping and spinning before bolting into the trees. Boo—some kind of black lab mix from my best guess—is more reserved. She sniffs me, then nuzzles her head into my thigh.

Once the dogs are settled, I put away my tools from the morning's errands and head to the workshop. Tucked among the trees behind the house sits the modified two-car garage. The midday sun streams through the floor-to-ceiling windows, casting the shop in warm light. I fire up the heater and begin sanding a table made of wood reclaimed from the floor of the now demolished bowling alley.

The scent of fresh sawdust hangs heavy in the air. It's one of my favorite smells, always reminding me of my dad, even though it's been years since we were in a workshop together. Butter dozes lazily in front of the heater while Boo lies on a pillow, eyes open and alert, faithfully watching over me.

Hours pass before a pang of hunger and the buzzing of my phone snap me out of my concentration. Out here in the shop, I can lose myself in my work, focusing on the task at hand, and not notice I've worked through lunch or dinner, sometimes even well into the night. Today, it seems I only missed lunch.

Glancing at the phone's screen, I see those two dreaded words, "*unknown number*," glaring back at me as the phone vibrates on the table. I pull off my respirator mask and work gloves, then press the button to send the call to voicemail.

Shaking the excess sawdust from my hair, I wait for the caller to leave a message. I wait…wait…wait. After more than a full minute, the phone pings with a new voicemail.

"Frank? Uh, hi. My name is Bennett Oliver. Most people mix it up and think my name is Oliver Bennett. It's not. It was a deliberate choice by my mom. She's a big Jane Austen fan. [throat clears] Anyway…um…I'm calling because I just moved back to Cherry Tree—although it's been thirty years, so it's not *really* like I'm moving back. I was nine when my parents got divorced, and

I... ugh, why am I telling you this? ... So, I've been working on fixing up my mom's old house. You might remember her: Cheryl Murphy? Though, it was Cheryl Oliver back then. She moved to Petoskey a few years ago and the house has been pretty much empty since then. Unfortunately, I'm a little green when it comes to home improvement, and I seem to have hit a snag with the water heater—the snag being that it doesn't work and now it's leaking water all over the floor. I called a plumber, but they told me it would take two days to get someone out here. I asked my neighbor if she could recommend someone, and she said I should call you. She's about eighty years old though, so I'm not sure she was the right person to ask. Anyway, uh, if you think you might be able to help me with my...situation, would you mind texting me back? Or if you can't...well, I guess either way, let me know. Thanks. Um, bye."

I shake my head, trying to recall what Evelyn had told me while I was fixing her porch. I vaguely recall her saying something about a man and his daughter moving into the old house next door to hers. If this Bennett Oliver guy is who she'd been talking about, and he really doesn't have any experience fixing up old houses, then he's definitely in over his head.

I text him back: «Send a pic, please.»

When my phone buzzes a moment later, I open the text and gasp, promptly dropping the phone to the floor. Retrieving it, I find myself not staring at a leaky water heater, as I'd expected, but at a stunningly handsome face.

The man in the photo is white with light skin and wavy, caramel-colored hair, long enough on the top that if it weren't tamed by styling products, would probably flop into his eyes. His lopsided smirk and a dash of pale freckles across his high cheekbones give him an almost boyish look. The creases at the corners of his bluish-grey eyes, and the lines bracketing his mouth give him up for being older, maybe around my own age.

I only notice I'm staring at the photo when Boo nudges me with her nose. Shaking my head, I text back.

«I meant a pic of the water heater. So I can see what tools I need to bring.»

Almost immediately, a string of texts from Bennett comes through.

Oh my god!!!!!

How embarrassing!!

I was wondering why you wanted a pic of me.

I'm so sorry.

Hang on a minute. I need to go downstairs to take a pic.

I chuckle to myself as I read each new message. Taking pity on him, I text again.

«Actually, don't worry about it. Just send me your address.»

Receiving his next text, I instantly recognize the address. The Murphy house is a gingerbread-style Victorian with delicate embellishments and a high-pitched roof, light yellow with forest green shutters. It's one of the oldest houses in Cherry Tree. Time and weather have faded the paint to a dull yellow-grey, and the shutters are tattered, but I can remember the house looking quite stunning in its heyday.

Given the age and condition of the house, this guy—who claims not to know much about home repair—is in trouble. *Oh boy.*

I respond: «15 minutes.»

I grab some tools, my jacket, and the sandwich from Evelyn before heading out. Fourteen and a half minutes later, I'm knocking on Bennett Oliver's door.

CHAPTER 2

BENNETT

"Oh thank god!" I practically shout as I fling the front door open, relieved that help has arrived. My eyes lock on the man I assume is Frank, and all of my thoughts scatter like marbles dropped on a tile floor. His eyes are a rich chocolate brown, his gaze on me sharp and a little intense. He's shorter than me, only by a couple inches, but where I'm lean, he's big—not hulking, but solid. Frank is muscular under his flannel shirt, I can tell, but it doesn't look like a gym body. It's probably been honed from years of manual labor: broad shoulders, a sturdy frame, and a little soft around the middle.

"Hi," I say when I recognize I'm staring. "Are you Frank?"

He nods, the tiniest hint of a smile on his face. He pulls off his knit beanie revealing dark hair, short around the sides and back, and a little longer and wavy in the front. It's flecked with a few strands of silver, more pronounced at his temples. He has light bronze skin and a short salt-and-pepper beard. I clear my throat.

"I'm sorry again about the picture. I'm so embarrassed! I should've known that's what you meant." Feeling my face flood with heat, I cover my cheeks with my palms before remembering my manners.

I thrust out my hand overzealously, and Frank shakes it, grip firm but not tight. His hands are warm and a little rough, further evidence that he works with them a lot. A gust of cold wind blows into the house, reminding me that we're still standing in the open doorway.

"Sorry! Come in!" Flustered, I say it too loudly, dropping his hand and stepping aside to allow Frank to pass. When the door closes behind us, Frank looks around, likely taking stock of the mess of moving boxes, hardware, and various piles of my daughter's toys.

"Sorry about the house," I say. "I've been trying to fix it up little by little since we moved in." Seeing it through Frank's eyes, I inwardly cringe. He doesn't seem to mind, shaking his head at the apology.

"So," I start, rocking on my heels. "Evelyn said that you don't—"

Frank turns his full attention to me, eyes narrowed.

"Actually," I say, running a hand through my hair. "Never mind. Let me hang up your coat and then I'll show you the water heater."

The stairs creak loudly as we descend into the basement. I pull strings to illuminate bare lightbulbs as we make our way to the far corner. When we reach the water heater, Frank produces a small flashlight from his pocket and shines it all around, first on the water that has gathered on the floor, then on the heater itself. He crouches to take a closer look, and my eyes instinctively go straight to the waist of Frank's pants, half expecting a dose of plumber's crack. But his shirt and pants stay exactly as intended. I internally scold myself. *Grow up, Bennett.*

Frank pokes around, shining the light here and there while I stand awkwardly, not sure whether I should stay and watch, or leave Frank alone to work. Before I can decide, Frank stands and pulls out his phone. He types for a moment, then turns the phone to face me.

«Drain valve issue. Could be faulty. Maybe bad installation.»

My face prickles with heat. I'd installed the new water heater a week ago, proud of myself for being able to figure it out. Frank doesn't seem to notice he's mildly insulted my handiwork.

«I'll work on it and come up when I'm done.»

I've been dismissed. Leaving Frank to his work, I amble back upstairs.

It shouldn't bother me—and it doesn't, mostly. Evelyn told me Frank doesn't speak, communicating either by text or the notepad on his phone. She also said he likes being left alone to work. I understand that—but still, I'd been hoping, just a little, that he'd want me to stay. I don't really know why, it's not like I can help. Given my experience, staying out of the way is probably for the best. I'd only distract Frank by trying to make conversation. Still, since the move back to town, I've been so wrapped up in research work, fixing the house, and taking care of my six-year-old daughter, I've been starved for time with other adults. It's just as well he doesn't want me to stay though—Libby will be home from school soon and I should clean up the paint roller and brushes before she can get her hands on them.

The moment I finish washing the brushes and drying my hands, Libby bursts through the door, tracking dry leaves and mud over the hardwood floor.

My heart swells as she launches herself into my open arms, nearly sending me tumbling backward onto the floor. She hugs me tightly, then goes boneless, her indicator she's ready to be set down so she can bounce from place to place like a spinning top.

"How was school?" I say and sign to her.

"Normal," Libby signs back. Before I can ask any follow up questions, she's off again, her attention already on something else. For a little while, I'd forgotten Frank was here, but the open basement door—and Libby's curious gaze—quickly reminds me.

I tap Libby on the shoulder to get her attention. She's almost completely deaf in one ear, and moderately deaf in the other. She has hearing aids but she's not used to wearing them, saying they make her ears hurt. Every time I suggest trying to wear them, it's a toss-up whether she'll comply or throw a fit. For now, she's much happier without them. She can hear very loud noises, or the occasional "LIBBY!" that I reserve for when she's about to do something potentially dangerous.

Once she's looking at me, I say and sign, "A man is here to fix the water heater in the basement."

Libby nods, then turns her focus back toward the stairs.

I tap her shoulder again. "He'll come up when he's finished. Let's leave him alone, okay?"

Libby nods once more, but still doesn't move. Finally, I take her by the arm and lead her away from the door, closing it behind us. I steer her to the kitchen and hand her a graham cracker from the pantry.

"The man in the basement is named Frank," I tell her as she eats. "He can hear, but he doesn't talk."

Chewing on a mouthful of cracker, Libby contemplates this for a moment, then sets the cracker on the table to free her hands to sign.

"He doesn't talk?" she asks.

"No," I respond.

"How do you know his name is Frank?"

"Evelyn told me."

Libby breaks off a piece of graham cracker, dropping crumbs all over the floor. I try not to picture the crumbs falling between the floorboards, inviting ants to a cracker buffet. She puts a large piece in her mouth, chewing slowly and staring off at nothing in particular, clearly deep in thought.

"If he doesn't talk, how does he order a pizza?" she asks.

I smile at that. I can see her trying to work out how Frank communicates with others, and in her six-year-old brain, ordering pizza is what she thinks of. I love this—learning how a child's mind can take a complex idea and break it down to something more manageable.

"He probably orders pizza with an app on his phone. When he needs to say something, he texts, or types on his phone and shows it to the other person."

"So, he talks," Libby signs, "but not with his mouth. Like me."

"Yes, that's right," I respond. "I should have said that he's nonspeaking."

Libby shrugs, swipes the rest of her cracker from the table and walks away, leaving a trail of crumbs behind her, clearly finished with this conversation.

Fifteen minutes later, the basement door swings open and Frank emerges, tools in hand. The knees and bottom half of his jeans are wet, but he seems unbothered. Pulling his phone out of his back pocket, he types quickly, then shows me.

«All fixed.»

"Great!" I say. "So, I guess it was bad installation after all."

Frank nods, then shakes his head, as if changing his mind.

«It was mostly right. Just a small adjustment. Very common.»

"You're just being nice," I say, rubbing a hand over the back of my neck. "You can say my handiwork is crap. I won't be offended."

Frank starts typing again, then stops, then starts again.

«Most people wouldn't even know where to start. You did great.»

"Okay," I laugh. "Now I know you're bullshitting me."

Frank's brows shoot up in surprise, eyes snapping to meet my gaze. He shakes his head vigorously, then types: **«I'm sorry. I didn't mean to insult you.»**

"Hey," I say, putting my hands up. "I'm only teasing."

He nods, but casts his eyes down. I wonder if he's not used to people joking around with him? He seems to be very serious, and from what Evelyn says, Frank doesn't socialize much, usually taking off as soon as a job is done.

"It's okay," I assure him, placing a hand on Frank's forearm where he's pushed up his sleeves. Frank stares at the spot where my hand touches his bare skin, and I quickly pull away, not sure if he likes to be touched or not.

"Sorry," I whisper, shoving my hand in my pocket.

Frank shifts on his feet, then catches my gaze. My throat goes dry and I swallow hard. We lock eyes for what must be a thousand minutes.

"I—," I start, but a small hand tugging my sleeve snaps me out of my trance. Libby's holding onto my shirt and staring at Frank.

"Hey, bunny," I say, lifting her, then arranging her on my hip so she has both hands free.

"Who is that?" she signs. Realizing I can't answer while holding Libby with both hands, I begin to shift her to free up my right hand so I can at least fingerspell. But before I can, Frank sets down his tools and begins to sign.

"My name is F-R-A-N-K."

Libby stares at him, eyes wide with surprise. She wiggles delightedly in my arms and I set her down so she can sign more easily.

"What's your name?" he asks, kneeling so they're eye to eye.

"L-I-B-B-Y," she fingerspells for him.

Frank smiles warmly and a little tingle of nerves flutter in my stomach.

Chill, Bennett. It's because he's being kind to your daughter.

"I fix things in houses," Frank signs. His dark eyebrows furrow in concentration as he signs, focusing on the words as if it takes a great effort to remember each one. His signing skills seem rusty, like he doesn't do it very often. And unlike a lot of people who sign, he doesn't move his mouth to mimic the movements of speaking while he does it.

Libby nods. "I'm six."

"Me too," Frank signs enthusiastically, and Libby giggles. "Okay, six plus thirty-two."

Libby laughs again, covering her mouth with her hands.

Frank puffs his chest out slightly, beaming like he's proud of himself. His gaze flicks to me, then immediately back to Libby. He points to himself, then gestures over his shoulder with his thumb, indicating that he's leaving.

Libby makes the sign for *stay* to Frank, but he shakes his head and makes an exaggerated sad face. He holds up two fingers, then makes the sign for *dog*.

"Dogs!" Libby replies excitedly. "Can I see your dogs?"

Frank pulls out his phone and clicks around, turning it to show a photo of two adorable dogs. He points to the sleek black one with a white patch stretching from chin to chest.

"B-O-O," he spells.

He points to the second dog, who at first looks dark grey, but on closer inspection, is black with white fur sprinkled in. The dog has patches of light brown, and one solid black patch around one blue eye, while the other eye is a honey brown. She should look like a chaotic mess, but all of it works together to make an utterly charming-looking dog.

"B-U-T-T-E-R," Frank spells.

Libby wrinkles her nose at the name.

"Butter?" I ask.

Frank shrugs without further explanation.

"Do they know that's what they're called?" Libby asks.

She waits as Frank scrubs his chin in thought. I'm surprised her mind has jumped to such a complicated question. Or maybe, in the mind of a child, the question of whether a dog who's never heard its owner call it by its name isn't complicated at all.

"Probably not," Frank finally replies with a silent chuckle.

"Can I pet them?" Libby asks.

"Yes. Soon, okay?"

"Okay, bye." Libby bounces around a bit, then runs back to the living room, where she plonks herself down on the sofa and turns on the TV. Suddenly self-conscious, I scuff the heel of my shoe on the floor where I'd dripped paint earlier.

"Well," I say. "That's my daughter. She hasn't quite mastered the art of a graceful exit."

Frank nods, giving me a small smile.

"Beautiful," he signs, then drops his gaze, the tips of his ears turning bright pink.

"Yeah," I agree. "Hey, I didn't know you knew ASL. I feel bad for not asking. You can sign with me, if that's better for you."

Frank pulls his phone out and types, but this time, instead of showing me his screen, my own phone buzzes with a text.

«I prefer typing when I can. I'm not so good at signing.»

"No? You seem pretty decent to me."

«Not many people to practice with around here. I don't know anyone in town who knows ASL except for a couple of teachers, but I don't see them much.»

"Well, now you know two more." I smile at Frank, then give him a wink. *A wink? Am I trying to flirt with him?*

No, I tell myself. The only people I've seen this past week are Libby, Evelyn, and the tattooed barista at the coffee shop. I just need someone to talk to. A friend.

Frank nods, but I can see the corners of his mouth tipping up ever so slightly.

I follow as he walks out onto the porch. He starts down the steps, and I feel a tug in my gut, like I don't want him to leave.

"Hey, Frank?" I call.

He looks back over his shoulder.

"What do I owe you for your troubles? I forgot to ask earlier."

He stops, then turns to face me, brows furrowed like he doesn't understand the question.

"I mean, I don't usually carry cash on me, but tell me how much and I'll bring you cash. Or Venmo? PayPal?"

Frank continues staring, mouth slightly open as I ramble on.

"It's just that you totally saved me today," I say. "I don't think I could handle two more days of giving Libby cold baths and—"

Frank holds up a hand to stop me from talking, shaking his head. He sets down his tools to free up his hands. "I don't take money for little things like this."

"Oh, right," I say. "Evelyn told me. But I'd like to give you something." *Ugh, chill, Bennett.* "I mean, something like..."

Frank's watching me with something like amusement in his eyes, like he enjoys seeing me get rattled.

"How about a beer or coffee sometime?" I offer. "My treat."

He frowns, drawing his brows together, like he's not sure what language I'm speaking. My face heats despite the chill in the air, but I press on.

"I haven't been here long, and don't have any friends," I explain. "Well, except for Evelyn, but I think she's in bed by eight o'clock most nights. And Lucy at the coffee shop—although I don't know if a barista learning your regular drink order counts as a friend." I chuckle nervously.

"Friends?" Frank signs.

"Yeah. I'd like to be friends with you…if you want, that is."

As he studies me, I push dry leaves around with the toe of my shoe. Evelyn said Frank keeps to himself. Maybe he doesn't want to be friends with me. Maybe he's trying to come up with a way to let me down gently.

"Or not," I say, trying to act nonchalant to hide my embarrassment. "It's fine, really."

Finally, Frank nods slowly.

"Is that a *yes*?" I ask, my voice painfully eager.

Frank nods more resolutely this time and my chest flutters with joy.

"Great! I'll text you soon."

I watch him back out of the driveway and disappear down the street before heading back inside, smiling to myself as I shut the door.

CHAPTER 3

FRANK

Friend. Friend. Friend.

The word ricochets in my head like a pinball. It's been a long time since I've had a friend, a *real* friend. I have acquaintances, sure, and a lot of people in town *call* me a friend. But friends talk to each other, confide in each other, lean on each other.

I try to remember someone, *anyone*, I genuinely talk to, not just someone who talks *at* me. I admit, I'm not much of a conversationalist, usually giving short answers or nods. But that never seems to bother anyone, and people don't typically ask for more than that anyway.

As for confiding, people tend to tell me things—things I probably shouldn't know, things that anyone who enjoys gossip would love to hear. They talk to me about personal things, but rarely ask what I think. I'm an ear. Someone to listen without the obligation of a response. Sometimes—when people in town tell me things they should've kept to themselves, knowing I won't repeat it or even respond—I feel like a houseplant. I don't want to be a houseplant. But I don't want to offend anyone, or make them feel embarrassed or ashamed for confiding in me. So I lock their secrets away, or, more precisely, I tune them out, choosing instead to get lost in my own thoughts.

And as for friends leaning on each other, I'm just fine relying on myself, thank you very much. I'm a fully functional, self-sufficient adult who can take care of myself. Other people rely on me to fix things around their homes, to help with things they can't do on their own, or in one case, to move a fucking piano down two flights of stairs. But it's not that often that I need to ask someone else for help. I'm not opposed, or too proud. I simply don't need to.

Sighing, my hope deflates. As much as I want a real, honest-to-god friend, it's likely Bennett will turn out like most other people in town, chatting my ear off without really wanting my thoughts, without bothering to get to know me at all.

In town, I'm the unofficial Nice Guy. Cherry Tree's Mister Congeniality. It's easy to be called such things when you don't speak. In my head, I could be a real asshole and no one would be the wiser. That thought makes me chuckle. I'd like to think I'm not a jerk, but all the same, it gives me a little thrill to think I *could* be.

I'm pulled out of my thoughts by a new text message:

Bennett: Hi Frank. Thanks for helping me today. You're a lifesaver. I'll text you soon about coffee or whatever.

I pull into my driveway and stare at the screen long after it goes dark, thinking about Bennett, with his kind, blue-grey eyes and deft hands that sign confidently. Bennett, with the adorable daughter who made my heart melt the second I met her. Bennett, the beautiful man who'd seemed to genuinely want to talk to me. *God. Why am I so fixated on the first person who's shown me the tiniest hint of interest?*

I scrub a hand over my face and snap myself back to reality before getting out of the truck.

Several days pass, and I don't get any more messages from Bennett—not that I really expect to. Bennett asked me to hang out because he wanted to repay me for fixing his water heater. It was a moment of frenzied relief it had been fixed, that's all. He hadn't really meant it. Still, every time I get a text or call, my heart skips a little, hoping it might be him.

On Wednesday afternoon, I return home from a call to fix a broken fence where a large animal—most likely a bear—had knocked over a couple of posts. A sodden chill hangs heavy in the air thanks to a cold drizzle that's been steadily falling since early this morning, leaving the driveway and path to the house a muddy mess. I'd read that an ice storm hit the area just to the north last night and I count myself lucky that Cherry Tree hadn't been affected. In this town, there's never a shortage of the kinds of weather that could keep me busy helping people who are stuck, snowed in, or flooded.

I let Boo and Butter out and watch from the porch as they meander, padding over wet moss and sniffing every rock along the shoreline. Gusts of wind send leaves tumbling into the lake. After a few minutes, I whistle for the dogs to come back inside. I make sure to clean their dirty paws with an old towel before they get too far into the house.

I consider going to the workshop to finish the table I've been working on, but the thought of slogging out there, starting up the heater and waiting for the cold, damp room to warm up sounds dreadful today. Ultimately, I decide against it, choosing to stay in the warmth of the house with my dogs, and catching up on emails and online orders.

Fresh out of a hot shower, I'm pulling on a wool sweater—faded and fraying at the cuffs—when my phone buzzes with a call. Distracted by the name on the screen, I don't notice Butter, who has a tendency to get underfoot. I stumble, nearly falling on top of her, and land with an ungraceful thud on the couch. I check that she's okay, then glance back at my phone. My heart freezes when I see that my thumb has accidentally swiped the *answer* button instead of sending the call to voicemail.

I slowly press the phone to my ear and hold my breath. Bennett speaks, his smooth voice higher and more distressed than it had been the day we met.

"Hello? Frank? Um, I didn't expect you to answer. I figured it would go to voicemail. Although it's fine that you did. Good, I mean. God, sorry. I'm...I babble when I'm flustered."

I picture Bennett, flushed and running anxious fingers through his hair the way I'd seen him do the day we met.

"I'm sorry for calling you the day before Thanksgiving, and I wouldn't, except in an emergency. Not that this is a life-and-death type of emergency. Nobody's hurt or anything like that. Don't worry. It's just that I was supposed to take food to make dinner at my mom's house tomorrow, but she lives in Petoskey, where they had that ice storm. She's fine, but there are some trees and power lines down, and some of the roads are closed. So Libby and I are sticking around here for the holiday."

I listen to Bennett's voice, words hurried and frantic, almost running together in one long sentence.

"So, the emergency—and like I said, it isn't a life-or-death emergency—is that my stove isn't working. I've used it pretty much every day since we moved in, but today, the whole thing quit on me. I hate to ask you since I'm sure you have other things to do, but, well, I'm desperate. I'm hoping it's an easy fix, like maybe it came unplugged from the wall, in which case, I'd be embarrassed, but it would be fine."

While his rambling continues, I text Bennett, hoping he'll take a breath long enough to see the message.

«15 minutes.»

Bennett pauses mid-sentence. "Oh, fifteen minutes. That's...thanks. I didn't mean for you to drop everything and come now. It's not like I'm cooking a turkey today. I just need it for tomorrow morning. Really, it's okay if you..."

«20 minutes if you don't stop talking.»

Bennett laughs and my chest tingles, just a little.

"Okay, fine. I get it, I talk a lot. Seriously though, if it's more involved than a quick fix, don't worry about it. I'll deal with it after the holidays. Uh...okay. See you soon. Bye, Frank."

I smile like a goof long after I've disconnected the call. I continue to smile as I lace up my work boots, tug a beanie over my damp hair, and leave the comfort of my house, squelching through the sleet-soaked leaves toward my truck. All the while, I buzz with the excitement of seeing Bennett again.

When Bennett opens the door, his hair is disheveled, and the creases between his brows give away his rattled state. He's wearing perfectly tailored navy pants and a white button-down shirt with sleeves rolled up to the elbow—a stark contrast to the paint-splattered clothes he wore the first time we met. I have to force myself to drag my eyes away from Bennett's forearms, pale with a light dusting of caramel hair.

"My knight in shining armor!" He's probably trying for a light tone, but he sounds harried. "Thank you for coming so quickly."

I nod, following him inside.

"Libby just got home from her after-school ASL lesson," he explains, holding out his hand for my coat. Once he hangs it up, he continues to chat as we walk down the hall. I notice he isn't signing as he's talking.

"I was going to warm up a frozen lasagna tonight because I was getting ready for Thanksgiving dinner tomorrow." Bennett stops and turns so abruptly, I nearly collide into his chest. He doesn't seem to notice. "I meant to ask: should I sign with you when it's just the two of us?"

I shake my head and sign, "No. Thanks for asking."

"Okay," he says. "Anyway, I thought I'd make something easy, you know?

"Good idea," I reply.

"I thought so too," he agrees. "Until the stove quit working and now I have no way to make dinner."

I point in the direction of the kitchen—which I remembered from the last time I'd been here—and raise a questioning eyebrow.

"Oh, right. Sorry," he says. "You're not here to listen to me whine about dinner. This way." He leads me to the kitchen where a sad-looking pre-made lasagna—still partially frozen in its silver foil pan—sits on the counter. He quickly slides it back into the freezer.

I pull out a flashlight and inspect the stove. In my periphery, I see Bennett leaning a hip against the opposite counter, arms crossed lazily in front of his chest like he's planning to stay a while. Trying my best to ignore the tingly feeling of his eyes on me, I poke around, testing each dial and switch. The poor stove looks to be almost as old as me.

"So," Bennett says behind me. "I'm sorry I haven't called you about drinks yet. Since we moved, I've been doing a research project for another professor, and I have to get my syllabi ready for my classes that start in January."

I nod but don't turn around, afraid my face will give away all my emotions. I don't want him to know how much I'd been wanting to see him again, how hopeful I'd been that someone was interested in getting to know me. And my disappointment that I haven't heard from him.

Pulling the stove away from the wall, I kneel down and peer into the gap at the back. As I lean over, I self-consciously reach back and touch a hand to the waist of my jeans, checking that my shirt and pants are still where they should be. I'm not sure if Bennett's even looking at me, but knowing he's there makes me hyper-aware of my every movement. When I venture a glance over my shoulder, he's occupied with his phone, but looks up just in time to catch me. I quickly turn my focus back to the stove, my cheeks going hot.

"I should tell Libby you're here," he says. "She'll be so happy to see you."

I turn to face Bennett and cock my head, hoping to convey my question: *why?*

"Ever since she met you, she's been asking when she's going to see you again. I thought it was because you know ASL, but I think she just likes you."

I drop my chin to my chest, smiling to myself as warmth blooms in my chest. I've always liked kids, but they don't always like me. They either get bored because I can't really joke around with them, or they find it too tedious to have to wait for me to type. Still, I can't help but be excited to see Libby. She's the only kid I've ever met who seems to genuinely like me.

With my free hand, I hold up a hand with all five fingers extended, hoping Bennett understands.

"Five..." he says slowly, looking at my hand. "...minutes?" I nod. "Oh, sure. Yeah."

He goes back to his phone while I work. Two minutes later, Libby's footsteps pound excitedly across the hardwood floors through the house and come to a stop at the edge of the kitchen. I turn to see her tiny frame almost vibrating as she stands, waiting for me.

"Hi, Frank!" she signs with exaggerated glee. "I saw your truck outside."

"Hi." I sit back on my heels, wiping my hands on the knees of my jeans.

"What are you doing?" she asks, observing the tools in my hand.

"Trying to fix the stove so you can have dinner," I respond. "But it's not good."

"What is it?" Bennett asks, stepping closer, trying to peer around me to the back of the stove.

"Mice," I sign.

Bennett takes three steps back, nose wrinkled in disgust.

"Eww," he cries through a grimace. I have to turn away so he can't see me bite back a smile.

By contrast, Libby is wide-eyed, thrilled by the discovery. She shoves past me to take a look for herself. Turning around, she pushes out her bottom lip in disappointment.

"Where?" she asks.

"Gone," I say before switching to typing on my phone.

«Looks like they chewed through the wires a while ago. You're lucky this stove worked at all. Or that it didn't cause a fire.»

Libby ignores my typed response in favor of peering around me to look for mice. When Bennett reads my message, he slumps against the counter, the deeper meaning of the news hitting him hard.

"So, definitely not getting fixed tonight," he says grimly, not asking but stating a fact.

"No," I say. "Sorry."

Bennett sighs heavily and turns to Libby. "Pizza?"

Libby jumps up and down excitedly in response.

I turn back to the stove, double checking that it's unplugged, then push it back into place. Behind me, I hear Libby's hands moving frantically, but I can't see her to know what she's saying.

"Yes," Bennett says. "I think that's a good idea. Frank, would you like to come with us for pizza?"

When I turn, Bennett and Libby are both staring at me with matching eager expressions. I'm struck by how much they look alike. Libby has Bennett's big, bluish-grey eyes, caramel blonde hair—hers long and pulled in a messy ponytail—and a dimple in her right cheek.

Normally, I'd find a way to politely decline the offer. I tend to avoid loud, crowded places when I can. While there's nothing wrong with my hearing, I've gotten used to the peace and solitude of my home in the woods. Being in small, packed spaces exhausts me, and I usually end up with a throbbing headache by the time the check arrives.

But standing in the kitchen, the pair in front of me looking so hopeful, the last thing I want is to disappoint Libby. And, *okay*, I want to spend time getting to know Bennett. I rub the back of my neck, then nod once.

"Really?" Bennett's voice is tinged with disbelief, but he's grinning that wide, infectious smile that makes my heart skip. Libby claps excitedly, then runs straight to the front door where she pulls on her boots and coat in ten seconds flat. Bennett and I follow a little more slowly. He hands me my coat, then shrugs on his own dark green, wool peacoat that reaches his knees and looks like it was tailor made to fit his lean form. I tug my beanie over my hair and wait as Bennett helps Libby zip her jacket.

"Meet us at Sal's?" Bennett asks as I open the door to my truck. Sal's Pizza is just around the corner, a longtime fixture on Main Street, but I don't care for it. The pizza is fine, but the restaurant is usually crowded and loud, and I can imagine it being even more so the day before Thanksgiving.

"Reggie's," I sign, hoping they'll be up for a slightly longer drive. "Five miles down the road. Better pizza, and quiet."

"Sounds great. I'll follow you."

CHAPTER 4

BENNETT

Walking into Reggie's Pizzeria, I instantly know Frank made the right call. Where Sal's is bright, colorful, and loud, Reggie's is cozy, inviting, and best of all, quiet. The fireplace in the corner emits a warm glow across the room, and the dark wood accents and soft lighting give off more of a ski lodge feel. The restaurant is small, with only enough room for eight four-top tables. There's a long table in the back, next to which is a shelf with dozens of board games in various levels of shabbiness. It certainly isn't what I'd been expecting for a pizza shop off a rural Michigan highway in the middle of nowhere.

Unsurprisingly, Libby chooses the big table and immediately begins perusing the games. Frank sits across from me and slides off his coat and hat, running his fingers through waves of hair that had been flattened by his beanie.

"Hey folks, I'm Elisa," the waitress—a young Latine woman dressed in a crisp white button-down shirt and black pants—chirps as she approaches the table. She's pretty, with long black hair and bright red lipstick. When her eyes land on Frank, she lights up.

"Hi, Frank!" Elisa pinches him affectionately on the shoulder. He gives her a little nod and a tight-lipped smile. "And who are your friends?" she asks, turning to face me.

"I'm Bennett, and that's my daughter, Libby." I point toward the end of the table.

"Well, it's nice to meet y'all. And I see Frank picked the best table in the place."

She winks and elbows Frank, who looks down at the table, sliding his palm over the surface with something like affection. It's hard to tell in the dark of the restaurant, but I swear Frank's blushing. Elisa places menus in front of Frank and me, and a placemat filled with puzzles and games and a cup with assorted crayons in front of Libby. Once we order drinks, Elisa heads back to the kitchen.

"The waitress likes you," I say, once she's out of earshot. Frank's eyes blink wide in surprise, and he tilts his head to the side. "Did you see how she lit up when she saw you?"

Frank shakes his head and signs, "Don't think so."

"Come on." I nudge Frank's foot with my own. "She winked at you, Frank! Definitely flirting."

Frank pulls his phone out of his pocket and types.

«She winked at me because of the table.»

"I don't get it. What's the table have to do with anything?"

«I made this table.»

"Seriously?" I ask, my turn to be surprised. "You made this?"

Frank doesn't look up, only runs a finger over a knot in the center of the table. He nods so subtly, I almost don't catch it.

The tabletop is made of a thick slab of light wood with rough bark still intact on the long sides. There are knots in the wood around which the tree had grown, forming interesting, beautiful shapes. The table isn't perfectly rectangular, but slightly off, following the shape of the tree, rather than being cut into an unnatural shape. It's clear

Frank built this table to be strong and sturdy, but also to showcase the fragile beauty of the tree from which it was made.

My fingers trace the live edge of the table, taking in its rugged texture. As I marvel at the craftsmanship, I catch Frank watching me through dark lashes. A spark hums through my chest as I imagine his sharp eyes and rough hands crafting a huge piece of wood into such a magnificent piece of art.

"This is gorgeous," I say, my voice catching. I clear my throat. "I can't believe you made this. It's so..." Shaking my head, I let my words drift away.

Frank shifts, looking uncomfortable, his eyes dropping to his hands.

"I'm sorry," I say. "I didn't mean to get all weird about it. I'm just in awe."

Shrugging, Frank signs, "Don't be sorry. I..." He pauses, brow furrowed and lips twisting in obvious frustration. He types on his phone, then waits. My phone buzzes a moment later.

«I'm not good with compliments.»

«I tried to sign it, but I couldn't remember the word.»

"Frank!" I exclaim. "You deserve the compliment! You're really talented."

I'm gushing, I know. But what else can I do? I'm more than impressed by his work. The tree Frank used for the table had been handled with care and respect. He hadn't sanded off the gnarled bits, or cut off the beautiful bark. He'd put a huge knot of wood in the center of the table like he was celebrating the uniqueness, giving a subtle middle finger to anyone who would want to hide or get rid of the supposed imperfections.

"So, is this what you do for a living?" I ask. "I mean, when you're not being the town superhero?"

Frank rolls his eyes.

«Yes, I'm a woodworker.»

"Okay…" I say after a long moment. I glance at Libby who's happily coloring on her placemat, so I turn my attention back to Frank. "Tell me more."

«I mostly make custom furniture. Sometimes I make cabinets, butcher block countertops, things like that.»

«The handyman stuff is my way of getting out of the house so I don't turn into a recluse.»

Frank's downplaying his role as unofficial handyman around town and we both know it. There are plenty of other ways to get out among people that don't involve fixing water heaters or replacing the batteries in the smoke detectors of elderly neighbors.

"How did you get into that…the woodworking?"

«My father.»

My eyes glance at Frank, then back to my phone, then back to Frank, waiting for more. It's becoming clear that he isn't comfortable having real conversations with people, giving short answers and allowing the other person to carry most of the exchange. I gesture for him to keep talking. He looks unsure, but begins typing again.

«My dad was a carpenter. Roofs, house frames, that kind of thing.»

He pauses, watching me read the message.

"Go on," I say in my most encouraging voice.

«He started making furniture and custom pieces as a hobby. He really liked it, so he turned his hobby into a full time job.»

"And he taught you?"

«Yes.»

«It's fitting that I was named after him.»

Frank silently chuckles, then drops his smile, looking at me with an unreadable expression. I'm not sure if he's waiting for me to encourage him to keep talking, or if he wants the exchange to just end already.

"Frank," I say, leaning in. "Is this miserable for you?"

He blinks at me, his mouth open in surprise. He shakes his head vehemently.

"No," he signs. "It's not—" He shakes his head again, more at himself this time, then types on his phone.

«No, it's not miserable for me. But it must be for you.»

"Why would you say that?"

He shrugs. «Because conversations with me are very slow.»

"I'm in no hurry here. I'm asking you questions because I want to know more about you."

«Wouldn't you prefer to do the talking?»

I read the text twice, my mouth dropping open. "Are you making fun of me because I talk too much?" I ask.

"What? No," he signs. Clearly thrown, he tries to sign something else, but doesn't seem to know what to say.

"Hey," I say, resting my palm over his hands. "It's okay. I was only kidding." He stares at me, unblinking. "Talk to me," I tell him, and although I keep my voice soft, it comes out a little bit commanding. "Please?"

Frank sighs and picks up his phone again.

"You were telling me about how you got into woodworking," I remind him.

He nods and starts typing again. As he does, I glance at Libby, who's still engrossed in coloring a picture on her placemat.

«Yes, my dad taught me. But not right away. After high school, I went to college in Detroit. I was there for two years.»

«I was a biology major, because I love nature, plus I'd been good at it in high school. But I didn't like it in college. I didn't want to memorize chemical formulas and all that. I just loved being outside. I wanted to build things. Just like my dad.»

He pauses, looking at me. I nod for him to keep going.

«The whole time I was in college, I never felt like I fit in. It wasn't that people treated me badly. Mostly, they treated me like I wasn't there. I was invisible.»

"That sounds like it would be really lonely," I say. Frank runs a hand through his hair, keeping his eyes on his phone. "So what did you do?"

«I figured out that college wasn't for me. It was the middle of the semester. I packed up my stuff, dropped out of school, and moved back here. I asked my dad to teach me about woodworking. I already knew a lot from being with him in his workshop, but when I said I wanted to do this for a living, he really took the time to teach me everything he knew.»

I nod as I take in every word. "And the handyman stuff?"

«Dad was always helping others. I'm not sure how he started, but ever since I was a kid, he would take me with him to fix things around town, just like I do. He'd show me how things worked. It became part of our everyday life. After my parents moved away, I felt like I needed to keep it going. People need someone they can count on. I've always tried to be that person.»

"Aha!" I slap my hand on the table, causing Libby—who's still coloring on her placemat—to jump.

"You admit it," I say in a softer tone. "You *are* a superhero."

Frank shakes his head. "I'm not," he signs. "I'm a guy who fixes stuff."

"You," I say, wrapping my hand around Frank's arm, "are a hero to the people you help. And don't say you're not. Remember the other day, when my water heater was leaking? You came over right away and fixed it. If you think stopping water from leaking all over my basement and restoring our hot water isn't heroic, you're wrong. Hell hath no fury like a six-year-old who has to take a bath in cold water."

Frank drops his head into his hands, his shoulders shaking. When he looks up again, I catch his wide, radiant grin. He's laughing, and my heart leaps. It's the first laugh I've been able to coax out of the man, and all I want is to do it again and again.

Elisa reappears, smiling brightly as she brings our drinks. After she takes my order, she leans close, placing a hand on Frank's shoulder as he points at the menu. Frank seems oblivious to her flirtation.

"I'm telling you, man," I say once she's gone. "She *likes* you." Frank picks up his phone and starts typing. I wait, seeing the three dots appear and disappear. He chews on his lip as he types and deletes, types and deletes.

Libby tugs on my sleeve, then signs, "Daddy? Are you done with your grown up talk?"

Frank and I look at each other and chuckle. He pulls the Connect Four game off the shelf and sets it up on the table, then invites Libby to play. The two of them end up playing several heated rounds before the pizza arrives. He loses every round, of course. I can't help but notice that he never finished whatever it was he'd been typing earlier.

As I watch Frank and Libby, it strikes me how easily he can make her smile, and how easily she makes him smile in return. Between Frank, who says he needs more practice with ASL, and Libby, being six years old and still learning how to read and write as well as sign, the two of them are just about on an equal skill level when it comes to signing. But as they chat with each other, neither of them seems self-conscious about not being great at it.

A pang of something that feels an awful lot like regret hits me square in the chest. *Why hadn't I come back to Cherry Tree sooner? Why had I stayed in New York—the place where I'd been so stressed and unhappy while trying to raise a child alone—for so long?* I run a hand through my hair and sip my drink, trying to shake off the wave of melancholy that threatens to ruin my good mood.

The pizza arrives and the three of us eat our dinner in happy silence, enjoying the warmth of the restaurant and ease of each others' company.

As Elisa boxes the leftovers and prepares the check, I groan remembering my broken stove and the uncooked food at home.

"Ugh." I scrub my hands over my face in frustration. "Tomorrow is Thanksgiving and I can't cook anything."

Looking at me with a twinkle of amusement in his eyes, Frank shakes his head.

"Do you think I can make an entire dinner using a toaster oven and the microwave?" I ask. Frank immediately signs, "no."

I sink my head into my folded arms resting on the table. The buzzing of my phone catches my attention and I sit up slowly, glancing at the screen.

«You could cook dinner at my house.»

I blink at the message, not sure if I've read it correctly.

"What?" I ask, looking up at Frank.

He taps a finger on my phone screen, indicating the message he'd just sent. Then he signs, "You can cook dinner at my house."

"I couldn't ask you to do that for me," I say. "I-I mean, you've already saved me. Twice."

Frank taps the phone again, harder this time to make his point.

"But what about you? I'm sure you have plans already."

Sighing heavily, Frank replies:

«I'm pretty sure I can put off eating leftovers and watching bad movies for one day.»

I frown, and a feeling that's somewhere in the neighborhood of guilt fills me.

"Is that really what you're planning on doing for Thanksgiving?" I keep my voice soft, and I know it sounds pitying, but I can't help it.

Frank nods and his leg begins to bounce up and down. He pulls at a loose thread on the sleeve of his sweater before he picks up his phone.

«It's not really a special day for me. Besides, I always get custom orders around the holidays that keep me busy.»

He pauses and I'm about to speak, but then he starts typing again.

«I have some work to do on a vacation house a few miles from town. I could stay there if you want the house to yourselves. I wasn't trying to invite myself to your holiday.»

"Are you kidding me? I'd never ask you to do that. *Of course* I want you there. If my stove suddenly started working again, I'd ask you to come over to our house. You shouldn't be alone tomorrow."

«I'm always alone. It's fine.»

The words hang heavy in the air between us, and I've never wanted to hug someone as much as I want to hug Frank right now.

I'm sure he hadn't said it to garner sympathy. It was a simple statement of fact. Frank seems comfortable with himself, and with being alone, at least from what I can tell. And he's around people all the time with his work as a handyman. Still, thinking about what it's like for him at the end of the day—going home to an empty house, eating dinner alone, going to bed alone—makes me unbearably sad. He must see the emotion on my face because he texts:

«No need to frown. I only meant that it's not a big deal for me.»

I'm not sure which part isn't a "big deal"—not having plans for Thanksgiving or being alone most of the time—but what I *am* sure of is that I don't want Frank to be alone tomorrow. And I certainly don't want to make him leave his own goddamn house after so generously offering it up to me.

"No. Nope. No way." I shake my head vigorously. "I'm not casting you out like a stray dog. Besides, I've never been able to make decent mashed potatoes. They always come out too sticky. That'll be your job."

A smile slowly spreads across Frank's face and my heart swells. He shrugs, then nods once.

"Okay?"

"Yes," Frank signs.

"Yes, what?" Libby asks, breaking her attention away from coloring on the back of her placemat.

"We're going to make Thanksgiving dinner at Frank's house tomorrow."

"Really?" Libby lights up as bright as the sun. "Can we see his dogs?"

I raise a questioning eyebrow at Frank.

"Yes, the dogs will be there," he signs.

"Does this mean I'll get to see some more of your furniture?" I ask.

He shrugs. "Sure, if you want."

I almost laugh at his ability to sweep aside any interest in himself or his work so casually.

Frank excuses himself to use the restroom, and I seize the opportunity to pay the check while he's gone. The gesture earns me an annoyed huff when he returns.

As we amble toward the door, I elbow Frank.

"Last chance," I say, keeping my voice low, causing Frank to lean in close. He smells like sawdust and peppermint soap and I nearly lose my train of thought. "Uh, we can wait outside while you say goodbye to Elisa."

He shakes his head and signs, "No...thank you," with finality.

I shrug. I don't know whether he isn't interested in Elisa, or if he's not interested in women in general. He hasn't given me any signs either way. I suppose it's not my business. He doesn't seem to take any offense to my gentle teasing though.

Frank puts his hands up like he's about to sign something, then seems to change his mind and shoves them into his pockets. The other time I asked about Elisa, he'd looked like he was going to say more too, but he stopped himself.

Almost as if she'd been watching us—or rather, watching Frank—Elisa emerges from the kitchen just as we're walking out.

"Bye y'all, it was great to meet you!" Turning her gaze to Frank, she squeezes his arm and murmurs, "Bye, Frank. See you soon."

As we head to the parking lot, Frank ducks his head, and I have to suppress a laugh. Ignoring my teasing, he texts:

«In the morning, the work on the vacation house will take an hour or two, but not more than that. You can come over anytime. If you're not there by the time I have to go, I'll leave the door unlocked.»

"That's a lot of trust you're putting in me," I say with a smirk. "I promise I'll be good."

Frank stares at me for a long moment, then nods. He says goodbye to Libby with a fist bump and a flourish. When he looks back at me, the smile on his lips is small, almost shy. He thanks me for dinner before getting into his truck, and I wonder again, *What was he about to tell me? And why did he decide not to?*

Libby's exhausted when we get home. I help her brush her teeth, get her into pajamas, and put her to bed right away. As I flop on the couch to unwind, I find a text waiting for me.

Frank: «Thanks again for dinner. I had a good time.»

The message isn't anything profound or effusive, but my heart leaps in my chest anyway. I bite my lip to keep from grinning too widely. But why shouldn't I smile? Frank is my friend. At least I think so. *Isn't he?*

Bennett: Me too. I don't get out much these days.

Frank: «Yeah, me neither.»

I reread my own message, aware that I'm implying just getting out of the house made me happy. It did, but that wasn't all. It had been Frank's company—his calm, easygoing presence, his amusement at my overreactions, his willingness to open up and share things that he clearly doesn't talk about with many people, and his affability toward both myself and Libby.

Bennett: It was good to get out, but I really meant to say that it was good to be out with you. I like getting to know you.

Is it too much? Will Frank think I'm flirting with him? I don't mean to. I'm just trying to be a friend...*I think.*

My ex used to say I flirt with everybody without even knowing I'm doing it. I chew my bottom lip as I watch the three dots appear and disappear. Frank tends to do this a lot. It seems that by not having the ability to speak out loud, he puts a lot more thought into everything he says—every text, every sign.

Frank: «Me too.»

I smile to myself. Maybe he puts a lot of thought into his texts, but he's still a man of few words. The text that comes next is a location pin, along with a second text that says "gate code" followed by five numbers.

After a minute, my phone buzzes again.

Frank: «You might want to bring some toys or things for Libby to do. My house isn't really equipped for a kid.»

Bennett: Thanks for the heads up.

Frank: «See you tomorrow.»

Bennett: Goodnight, Frank.

Frank: «Goodnight.»

I'm smiling to myself until the moment I finally fall asleep.

CHAPTER 5

FRANK

I stare at the conversation on my phone for a long time. There was so much more I wanted to say to Bennett. It wasn't *just* that I had fun tonight. It'd been one of the best nights I've had in years. Bennett hadn't done all the talking the way most people do. He asked questions and pushed me to answer with more than my usual single-word responses. I'd been uncomfortable at first, but once I realized he was truly interested in what I had to say, the words flowed easily. And he never talked before I was done typing. It's strange how something that seems so small and insignificant can make such a big difference.

It's after ten o'clock when it dawns on me that if I'm going to have guests tomorrow, I need to do a little bit of cleanup. I always keep my house tidy, but I want it to feel freshly cleaned when they arrive. Plus, I need to burn off some of this nervous energy radiating off me. So, I scrub every surface in the kitchen until it looks new. I check the fridge, throwing out anything that's expired. I sweep and mop the floors, dust every surface of the living room, use a broom to bat away a couple of spider webs from the corners of the ceiling, and vacuum the rugs and couch to remove any lingering dog hair.

Butter and Boo watch in confusion, clearly not used to so much activity at night. Eventually they lose interest and fall asleep in front of the fireplace.

At two-thirty in the morning, I run out of steam and declare the house acceptable for company. Once I'm in bed, I toss and turn, the hum of excitement in my chest making sleep nearly impossible.

I must've fallen asleep eventually because I'm woken by Boo's cold, wet nose poking my hand, followed immediately by Butter jumping onto the bed and landing one paw directly on my crotch. I wince and try to bat her away, but she's too quick. She jumps down, spinning around once before running toward the back door—a clear sign she needs to go outside. Now.

It's eight o'clock—later than I normally sleep—and the dogs stare at me, none too pleased about the late hour. I let them out, then shuffle barefoot into the kitchen to make coffee.

I'm not sure what time Bennett and Libby will be coming over, but I've heard sometimes people start roasting their Thanksgiving turkeys at the crack of dawn. The thought of Bennett showing up any moment, turkey in hand, has me tingling with anticipation.

I pull on my work jeans and a black sweatshirt, and check my phone. No emergencies that need immediate attention...yet. *Thank goodness*. And no messages from Bennett.

A few days ago, I'd gotten a call from Jules Walker, the twenty-something from Chicago I've known since he was a toddler. Jules said he'll be bringing a couple of friends to stay at his parents' lake house for the Thanksgiving weekend. His parents live in the suburbs of Chicago, and own a modest-but-stylish vacation house in the woods just outside of Cherry Tree. They'd hired me years ago to check on the house twice a week and do any repairs or maintenance that need done while they're away. The Walkers used to come up at least once a month, spending several days, or even weeks, at the house. In the last few years though, they've been coming less and less, but Jules has been visiting more often, usually with his girlfriend, Evie.

I like Jules a lot. He's an influencer who has a pretty significant following on YouTube. He's gregarious and funny, and always radiates joy. He identifies as gender fluid, but still mostly uses he/him pronouns. I've never met anyone like him—someone so unapologetically himself—and I admire him so much for it. In the middle of the forests of northern Michigan, he stands out like a bird of paradise.

In all the years I've known him, he's always been so kind to me. He's more than ten years younger than me, but I think if he lived closer, we could actually be friends.

Any time Jules or his parents are going to be at the lake house, I stock up on some of their favorite snacks that aren't available in Chicago and bring them to the house as a little treat. I also stock the fridge with a few essentials: eggs, milk, cheese, and butter, along with some items to make an easy lunch or dinner. And once they go home, I'll come back and take out the trash, check all the doors and windows, and do anything else that needs done once they're gone.

Jules' text says that he and his friends will arrive early this afternoon. I'm at the house early to get everything ready so they'll have a comfortable, cozy place to rest after a long drive. I place some fresh flowers in a large mason jar of water on the counter, put the groceries in the fridge, along with a bottle of white wine—a local brand that Jules likes—to chill. I pull a small basket out of the laundry closet and fill it with the snacks I brought, along with some chips, pretzels, a bag of freshly ground coffee, and a couple bars of dark chocolate.

After that, I sweep the porch, clearing away the dead leaves and pine needles that litter the walkway and steps. I turn on the heat, checking that it's working properly and warming up the house for their arrival.

On my way out, I leave a couple of lamps on and turn on the string lights that hang around the porch, giving the whole house a warm glow.

The Walkers don't ask me to do all of this, but I enjoy doing these small tasks for them. I like making a house feel cozy and inviting. It's something I'd always imagined doing at my own house for someone I love—a boyfriend or a husband.

On my way home, I stop at Cherry Tree's only coffee shop, aptly named Cherry Tree Café. It's not the world's best coffee, but the staff is always kind to me and the pastries are pretty good. I order for myself, then venture to ask via my notepad app whether Lucy, the young, tattooed barista, knows Bennett's favorite drink. The day we first met, Bennett had mentioned becoming a regular here.

I hadn't thought much about the idea of becoming a regular anywhere. I've lived in Cherry Tree my whole life. People in town have always known who I am, and usually know what I'm going to order without me having to do anything more than wave. I don't think I'd like to live in a big city where you could go to the same places every day for years and still be a stranger to most people.

With only a slight raise of her pierced eyebrow, Lucy hands over my usual black coffee and a vanilla latte with an extra shot of espresso for Bennett.

Deciding I should offer Bennett and Libby something to eat, I peer into the pastry case and am immediately overwhelmed. Having no idea what they'd like, I end up with eight assorted pastries for the three of us. I feel a little silly buying so much, but the thought of the two of them in my house—Libby playing on my floor, and Bennett cooking in my kitchen—fills me with so much joy that I don't care that I've bought too much.

The rest of the shops are closed and most people are getting ready for the holiday, leaving the quaint downtown quiet and peaceful. Heading to my truck, I enjoy the satisfying crunch of fallen acorns under my boots and the damp, cold breeze on my face.

I pull up to the house and my heart leaps at the sight of Bennett's compact SUV in the driveway. Slowly opening the front door, I can't help but smile as Libby, unaware of my presence, sits cross-legged on the floor petting Butter, whose tail thumps excitedly against the hardwood. I glance toward the kitchen to see Bennett unloading a bag and placing groceries in the fridge.

Butter must smell either me or the pastries because she bolts to the front door, stepping on Boo, and nearly knocking Libby over. I have to hold the drink carrier high above my head to keep the dogs from jumping up and sending the coffees to the floor. Libby's eyes go wide and she beams excitedly when she sees me. Jumping into the mix, she bounces around me as excitedly as the dogs.

"Good morning," Bennett says, grinning widely as he approaches. To Libby, he signs and says, "Let's give Frank some space, okay?"

He takes the drink carrier from my hand, and urges her to back up so I can make my way into the house.

Placing the pastry box on the dining table, I kneel to pet the dogs and give Libby another fancy fist bump. It's becoming our standard greeting, and it warms my heart to know we have something special, something just between the two of us.

"Morning," I sign to Bennett, as I walk into the kitchen. I pluck a drink from the carrier and hand it to him.

"Is this for me?" he asks.

"No, it's for Libby," I deadpan. "Black coffee, extra strong, right?"

Bennett stares at me for a moment, and I wonder if he can tell I'm joking. But then he laughs and I'm flooded with joy. He has the kind of eyes that close almost entirely when laughs or smiles. I feel immensely proud to be the one to cause it.

"You little shit," he says to me.

The instant Bennett says it, his eyebrows shoot up and he covers his mouth with his hand. We both glance at Libby, who's occupied with the dogs. I'd noticed Libby's hearing aids in her ears when I came in, but I guess she isn't paying us any attention because it seems she didn't hear Bennett. Relief washes over his face.

Libby scratches Butter's head, then signs, "Daddy said a bad word," as if talking to the dog. "Now he owes me an ice cream." She looks over her shoulder and gives us both a wicked grin.

Nodding solemnly, Bennett looks chagrined. "Yes, you're right. I'm sorry."

Libby turns back to the dogs and continues petting them.

To me, Bennett mouths the word *fuck*, then shakes his head. Without thinking, I burst out laughing. It's a quiet, rough, raspy sound like a muffled chainsaw, and I hate it. I laugh so rarely that the sensation of my voice working in my throat feels foreign to me. It's seldom enough for me to use my voice, especially in the company of others, that I forget to hide it now.

Bennett's eyes go wide, and when I realize why, my face goes hot and I snap my mouth shut.

"Frank!" he exclaims. "You...your voice! I thought...," he sputters.

I scrub a hand over my eyes, trying to hide my face.

"I thought your voice didn't work. But it's there, isn't it?" His own voice is full of kindness and wonder.

I squirm uncomfortably. My disability isn't something I'm ready to talk about with Bennett yet. Maybe one day, but not now. So instead, I shrug, avoiding his eyes.

"Drink your coffee," I sign.

Bennett must recognize my reluctance to talk about it, because he doesn't press any further. Taking a sip, his eyes close, and he smiles, a single dimple on full display.

"Is this a vanilla latte with an extra shot?" he asks. I nod. "How did you know?"

"I asked," I sign simply.

Bennett raises an eyebrow, and a mischievous little grin creeps across his face. "You asked about me?" *Oh god.*

My ears radiate heat. I need a distraction. The last sixty seconds has been too much, too exposing. I open the box of pastries, then type on my phone, mostly to avoid Bennett's gaze...and his question.

«I didn't know if you had breakfast, or what you'd like, so help yourself.»

«Or not. Up to you.»

"Thank you." He drags the word out slowly as he plucks a cherry turnover from the box. "That was really thoughtful of you." He eyes me like he's working out a complicated math problem.

Moving around the kitchen, I can feel Bennett watching me, can see his lazy smile out of the corner of my eye. The room feels thick with something that's either excitement or nerves. I distract myself by putting on some mellow holiday music over the speaker in the living room before texting Bennett.

«Sorry I wasn't home when you got here.»

"No problem," he says. "We got here a few minutes before you, so I was just putting everything away."

I nod and sip my coffee, walking around awkwardly, like *I'm* the guest, not Bennett.

"This kitchen is spectacular." Bennett motions around the room. "Did you do all of this?"

"Yes," I sign, ducking my head to hide my blush. The cabinets are white with warm grey accents, and the counters are custom butcher block, something I'd been immensely proud of when I finished them. I'd foregone upper cabinets in favor of live edge wood shelves on which my dishes, cups, and glassware are stacked. The appliances are top-of-the-line, one of the few indulgences I allowed myself when I built the house.

"In fact, this whole house is beautiful. How long have you lived here?"

I twist my lips in thought, running a hand over the salt and pepper stubble on my chin. "Ten years."

Bennett continues to look around in wonder. "Did you build it yourself?"

"Yes. Well, there was a house here before, but it was in bad shape. I basically started over. With help, of course."

"Well, I love it. Did you make the furniture, too?"

"Most of it. Not the sofa or the chairs, but almost everything else."

"Oh my god, Frank," Bennett says, giving me a playful shove on the shoulder. "You are ridiculously talented, you know that?"

I stare down at my hands, tugging at the cuff of my sleeve. I'm proud of the work I do, but sometimes it's hard for me to know whether people are actually complimenting my work, or just being nice. But Bennett's praise feels genuine.

"When I look around my own house," he continues, "all I see is what needs to be fixed. Sometimes it gets so overwhelming."

"Your house isn't that bad," I offer.

"Yeah? How about we swap? I'll stay here since it's pretty much perfect, and you can fix up my house."

"No, thanks," I say. Then, because I can't sign it the way I want to, I text:

«I don't want to take away the feeling of accomplishment you'll feel when it's done.»

Bennett snorts when he reads my text.

"That's bullsh—" He cuts himself off, then says, "I mean, that's baloney, and you know it."

I give him a little smirk. *What are we doing? What am I doing?*

Bennett watches me for a moment, his brows furrowed. And like before, it feels like he's working something out about me in his head, but he doesn't say anything more.

"So do you need any help in the kitchen?" I ask, trying to change the subject.

"I'll have to start getting the turkey ready soon," Bennett says, "but it's not very big, so it won't need to cook that long."

I switch on the TV, putting the Thanksgiving Parade on in the background as we get to work. We settle into an easy rhythm: Bennett asking where to find things like aluminum foil, spices, and pans, while I locate items and do whatever I can to be helpful without getting in the way. Eventually, he seems fine on his own, and probably prefers to take control of the cooking, so I leave to take a shower.

When I emerge from the bathroom, hair damp and face flushed, the incredible scents wafting in from the kitchen hit all of my senses at once. The sensation nearly takes my breath away. It isn't any one particular smell, but rather, a mixture of herbs and spices, onion, garlic, and the warm, smoky aroma of the fireplace. It's been so long since I've been part of a real Thanksgiving dinner, especially one that's in my own home, I'm suddenly overwhelmed with memories.

The last time I'd been part of a home-cooked Thanksgiving dinner, my dad had tried to deep fry a turkey in one of those cookers we'd all seen on the internet. It was a disaster and he'd nearly burned the house down, so we ended up eating a pork roast mom had stockpiled away in the freezer, along with all of the usual Thanksgiving side dishes. It took forever to clean up the oil and burn marks from the driveway, but in the end, it was one of the best Thanksgivings I'd ever had. Thinking about it now gives me an unexpected sting in my eyes.

Bennett doesn't notice me coming down the hallway, so I lean against the wall and watch as he moves around the kitchen with purpose, placing pots on the stove in preparation for use, and checking recipes on his phone. I observe his long fingers as he expertly chops fresh herbs with a large knife.

"You know," Bennett says after a minute, not looking up as he peels a potato over a bowl, "I can feel you watching me."

I snap my gaze away as he turns to face me. Leaning a hip against the counter, he stares, and I wish a sinkhole would open up and swallow me whole. He smiles smugly.

"Come on," he says, holding out the peeler to me. "You do the potatoes while I check on the turkey."

A full minute of peeling passes. I'm squirming in my skin, embarrassed that I'd been caught watching Bennett, yet wanting so badly to keep on doing it. I try to tune out the thoughts and concentrate on the task at hand: *potatoes*. But every time Bennett brushes past me, all my focus goes out the window.

Once I'm done peeling, I chop the potatoes and add them to the pot of boiling water. When that task is done, I wash my hands, dry them on my jeans, then pick up my phone and type, turning it toward Bennett.

«Tell me about your job?»

For the next several minutes, we work in tandem, me making the mashed potatoes, and Bennett prepping the side dishes. All the while, he tells me about his job teaching English at the nearby community college, as well as doing historical research for authors. Bennett lights up with excitement when he talks about his work. Every now and then, goes into the living room to check on Libby and give her a little sample of what he's cooking.

"My ex couldn't understand why I'd want to move to the middle of Michigan and teach at a community college, when I could be teaching at a major university. Or why I do research for independent authors who don't have a lot of money rather than for big-name authors who could pay a lot more. He was always looking for every opportunity to make the most money, or the biggest boost to his career." Bennett doesn't say it with any bitterness, or even sadness. He states it as a simple fact, as if he were talking about the weather.

I stop what I'm doing and study Bennett. For a moment, he doesn't seem to notice.

"What?" he asks when he catches my eyes on him.

"You're..." I sign, then pause. "You're gay?"

"Yeah, you didn't know?" he asks.

I shake my head.

"I'm surprised Evelyn didn't tell you. That woman loves to tell other peoples' business."

"She's lonely and likes to make conversation," I say, suddenly feeling the need to defend the poor old woman. "But you're right, she does."

The more I think about it, the more I think maybe she *did* tell me, but I might've tuned it out, the way I always do whenever she gets to telling other peoples' business. It's why I don't tell her—or anyone else—anything about myself.

"Are you...okay with that?" Bennett asks cautiously.

I furrow my brow. "Yes, of course," I answer. I chew on my bottom lip and turn my attention to washing the cutting board.

Libby tugs on Bennett's sleeve to get his attention.

"Daddy, when is food going to be ready?"

"Not for a while," he answers. Libby huffs dramatically. "We're done with everything for now. There's not much else to do until the turkey is closer to ready."

"How about we go for a walk outside?" I suggest.

"Outside?" Libby repeats, wrinkling her nose.

"She's a city kid," Bennett explains. "She's not very outdoorsy."

I wave his comment away. "Come on. It'll be fun." I nudge Libby on the shoulder.

On the mat next to the door, three pairs of boots sit in a neat row: one pair of worn, brown work boots, one pair of classic black Chelsea boots, and one pair of sparkly, rainbow rain boots that are smaller than the others by at least half. I sit on the bench beside the door and pick up a boot while Libby watches closely.

Attempting to slide my foot into the boot, I tug and wince, wriggling my foot from side to side. Libby runs over waving her hands in the air, giggling wildly.

"Stop!" she signs.

I freeze, glancing between the boot and Libby a couple of times. I feign surprise to find that I'm trying to pull on her sparkly boot. She squeals with delight as I try one more time to pull it onto my foot, squeezing my eyes shut as I do. With a dramatic sigh, I take the boot off and set it on the floor, then sign, "I guess that one isn't mine."

I pass it to Libby, who puts it on right away, followed by the other boot, and then her jacket. Bennett and I follow, and soon, we're stepping out into the cold air. It's early afternoon, and remnants of the morning's drizzle have faded to a chilly mist. Every now and then, a ray of light pokes through the thick clouds, and the water droplets clinging to the few remaining leaves sparkle in the breeze.

Libby leads the way down the stairs of the back porch while Bennett cautiously brings up the rear. We amble along a dirt path that leads into the woods behind the house, shoes squelching as we step through piles of wet, dead leaves.

The dogs, who usually take off into the trees whenever I come outside with them, must sense something's different today, and stay close. Butter, following her instincts as a herding dog, circles us constantly, making sure no one gets too far ahead or behind.

We only make it a few yards from the house when I stop on the path. Butter intercepts Libby, keeping her from going any further. Libby turns, eyebrows furrowed in apparent confusion.

"Wait," I sign to Libby. "I need to give you something."

Libby skips back to me and waits while I fish the mysterious object out of my pocket. I gesture for her to open her palm. In it, I set a shiny, silver whistle—the kind coaches and gym teachers use—tied to a long, red cord.

She stares at the whistle, then glances at Bennett as if she's not sure what to do with it. He shrugs, looking as confused as Libby.

"It's a whistle," I sign. "It's very loud. Use it in case of an emergency."

"Emergency?" she asks. I start to sign, then pull out my phone instead, typing into the notepad. I want to make sure they both understand.

«Keep it around your neck when we're out here. If we get separated, if you get lost, see something scary, or if you get hurt, blow on it as hard as you can so we can find you. Keep whistling until someone comes.»

I turn the phone so they can both read it. I'm not sure how well Libby can read, and I hope Bennett will either confirm that she understands, or sign to her in case she can't. When they finish reading the note, I ask Libby, "Do you understand?"

She gives me an exaggerated nod, then puts the whistle around her neck.

"I have one, too. See?" Reaching inside the collar of my shirt, I pull a dark green cord revealing an identical silver whistle. "Want to try yours out?"

Instead of answering, she sticks the whistle in her mouth and lets out an ear-splitting trill. The dogs bark, Bennett covers his ears, and Libby's own eyes go wide with astonishment. She's not wearing her hearing aids like she was earlier, but the whistle is loud enough to surprise her. She beams with something like joy, or maybe pride.

"Okay?" I ask. She gives me a thumbs up.

My eyes flick to Bennett and I wonder if he thinks I'm overstepping by giving Libby a whistle. But there's only warmth, a kind of glow that I recognize as gratitude—not because I'd given her a gift, but something deeper than that. Maybe because he knows I want her to be safe. I understand that someone with a disability might need another way to communicate in an emergency. I can't help but feel protective of Libby, and my heart fills with relief that Bennett seems to understand.

I lead them a little further, not venturing too far from the house. My plan is to stick to the path that outlines the surrounding trees. To our left, a couple of squirrels chase each other up a towering tulip poplar, chittering as they scrabble up to the top. I turn around in time to see Bennett timidly stepping over a fallen tree and frowning, clearly not comfortable with walking in the woods. He catches me looking and gives me a thumbs up, pasting a tight smile on his lips. I chuckle silently and shake my head.

We continue for a few minutes, until we round a bend and encounter a patch of wet, moss-covered rocks littered with fallen pine cones. Bennett, who's wearing the wrong kind of shoes for this terrain, slips, pitching sideways. Beside him, I reach out, catching him by the waist and steadying him. I let my hand linger just a touch too long before pulling it away, glaring at the offending patch of rocks. *How dare you?* I think, internally scolding the rocks.

"Thanks," Bennett says, his face reddening. "I don't think this is quite my thing."

"You could do it," I sign. "You just need practice. And the right shoes." I looked pointedly at his expensive-looking boots, out of place in this setting. Still, I have to admit they look good on him.

"I didn't know hiking would be on the agenda!" he exclaims, throwing his hands in the air cartoonishly.

"I'm sorry," I say, suddenly worried I've hurt his feelings. "I was kidding."

I'm not good at joking around, never have been. So much of friendly teasing is wrapped up in voice inflection and facial expressions. I can't use my voice, and it doesn't help that I don't wear a lot of emotion on my face, preferring to keep my feelings tucked away in my own personal vault. I keep my eyes glued to the path.

"I know." Bennett pinches my elbow lightly and winks, sending a thousand sparks of electricity bursting through me and leaving me dazed.

Once I can think again, I type into my phone.

«Actually, I don't like leaving the oven on when I'm not in the house. I could hang out here with Libby for a bit longer, if you don't mind going back to keep an eye on things.»

Relief eases the lines around Bennett's mouth, and he exhales loudly when he reads the message.

"Are you sure?" he asks, already turning to go.

«Yes. We'll stay close to the path so you can see us from the house. Butter will keep her from wandering off.»

«Libby has her whistle if anything happens.»

"Thank you for that, by the way." He bumps his shoulder against my own.

I shake my head, waving a hand like I'm shooing a fly.

"No, seriously." Bennett's gaze locks on mine, and the sincerity on his face freezes me in place. "That was so smart and thoughtful."

I stare at him for far too long, only breaking eye contact so I can type on my phone.

«I know what it's like to feel vulnerable.»

I think of my abuelo, who'd first given me a whistle when I was six years old. So much of my carefree childhood had been stripped away from me, replaced by headaches, anxiety, doctors' tests, hospital stays, surgery, recovery, and finally, the realization that my brain could no longer make my mouth form the words I wanted to say. *Verbal apraxia* was what the doctors had called it—a result of a surgery for a brain tumor that had caused an interruption between my brain and the muscles needed for speech. Papi had watched as I struggled for months through speech therapy, trying to make words again, despite the bleak prognosis that I'd likely never regain my ability to speak.

When Papi gave me the whistle, it was a reawakening of sorts, like a tiny beam of sunlight wrenching its way through a storm. I irritated everyone around me with the annoying trill, but I didn't care. Being able to make loud noises with my mouth again made me feel free in a way I hadn't since before my surgery.

"I'm sure you do," Bennett says, breaking me out of my thoughts. "That's why it means so much that you did that for her."

I blush, tucking my hands into my pockets while he explains to Libby that he's going back to the house. She only half pays attention, more interested in poking at worms with a stick. Bennett shudders as he watches her, and I chuckle before gesturing for him to go.

CHAPTER 6

BENNETT

When I reach the back porch, I tug off my muddy boots and leave them by the door. The soft drizzle has returned and I'm beyond grateful that Frank gave me an excuse to come back. The warmth of the house envelops me in a welcoming embrace and I shake off the cold droplets of mist from my hair. Checking the oven, I find the turkey still slowly baking away. It still has another hour to go and most everything else is either ready or needs to be done just before the turkey comes out. So, with nothing else to do, I snag a blanket from the back of the couch, wrap it around my shoulders, and go back outside, settling myself on one of the Adirondak chairs.

Frank and Libby are far enough away that I can't tell exactly what they're doing, but I can make out Libby's movements, jumping, running, and exploring, while Frank points things out and signs to her. The dogs are walking around, but don't go very far. Boo keeps a silent, watchful eye on them, while Butter circles the perimeter, nudging Libby when she strays too far from Frank.

As I watch, my mind swirls around Frank—his kindness, his thoughtfulness. I wonder about his disability, what it must be like to not be able to speak. Has he had this disability his whole life? Were people nice to him, or was he bullied as a kid? Does he live out here all alone because he wants to avoid people? He'd said he does handyman work to keep from being a hermit, but living in the woods was a choice he made. He could live in town and do the handyman work just as easily. In fact, it would probably be much easier if he did.

My thoughts eventually wander to his dating life. I haven't known him long, but he hasn't mentioned a partner. He doesn't seem interested in Elisa, even though it's clear she's interested in him. And the way he looks at me sometimes...

Stop it, Bennett. That's none of your business. Still, Frank's a catch: handsome and thoughtful with a talent for being able to make beautiful, functional works of art with his hands. *Those hands.*

The sight of Frank and Libby heading back pulls me out of my thoughts. My heart melts seeing the two of them, Libby holding Frank's hand comfortably while the dogs follow closely behind. They stomp up the stairs to the back porch, shoes and pants muddy. On her way inside, Libby hands me a handful of dried wildflowers, long, yellowing pieces of wild grass, and a few sticks, which I decide to use as a makeshift centerpiece.

Inside, the blast of warm air, the amazing smells of dinner, and Libby's excited storytelling hit all of my senses at once. It's a feeling of perfection, a feeling of rightness.

Frank apologizes at least three times for the state of Libby's clothes and shoes, but I wave it off. I reassure him that as a parent, I learned long ago to always carry at least two spare changes of clothes for Libby. I grab my backpack of emergency clothes, sling it over my shoulder, and march Libby into the bathroom, returning a few minutes later with a pile of damp, muddy socks and pants, and a daughter in a fresh outfit. She immediately bounces to the couch where she curls up under a blanket and begins reading a book, something about a squad of mouse detectives.

"Dinner's almost ready," I tell Frank. "How about you go clean up, while I finish things here? Then you can help me with drinks and setting the table."

Frank nods and goes to his bedroom to change. While he's gone, I smile to myself thinking about how I'd so easily made myself at home here. And how Frank seems to have no problem with me ordering him around in his own home like we've known each other for years. I kind of love it.

Ten minutes later, Frank emerges wearing dark, fitted jeans and a soft, moss-colored wool sweater. His face is shiny and flushed, like he's just washed it, and his hair is damp and tousled, the ends curling around his face.

"Well," I remark, letting my eyes trail slowly from Frank's wool socks up to the drop of water clinging to the end of one of his dark brown curls. "You certainly clean up nice."

Frank's cheeks flood to a sweet shade of pink, but he keeps his focus on the task of filling three glasses with water and placing them on the table. I hand him a bottle of wine, and he opens it, pouring two glasses as I place the last of the side dishes on the table, followed by the turkey.

Half an hour later, full and content, Frank and I linger at the table while Libby—who asked to be excused seven minutes into dinner, declaring herself full—sits on the couch with her iPad, watching her favorite kids' program where all the dialogue is in ASL.

Frank tries to insist on washing the dishes while I relax, but I refuse to give in, telling him several times that I owe him for letting me and my daughter crash his Thanksgiving. When he asserts that *he* owes *me* because he'd have spent the day eating leftovers and watching movies alone, we eventually agree that we both appreciate the kindness of the other and wash the dishes together.

I'm a fairly neat cook, cleaning as I go, so there aren't actually that many dishes to wash. Once the last plate is placed in the rack to dry, Frank and I shuffle to the couch where Libby's petting Boo who's curled up next to her. There's a football game on the muted TV but neither of us pays attention to it. Frank had briefly stolen glances at the TV earlier when the Detroit Lions were playing—a tradition in most Michigan households on Thanksgiving—but since then, it's been mostly ignored.

We clear the dining table and play a modified game of Uno in which instead of shouting "UNO!," the player has to make jazz hands when they're left with only one card. The game eventually dissolves into laughter, jazz hands become some kind of arm-flapping chicken dance, and cards end up flung all over the floor.

After a few rounds, Frank removes a homemade cherry pie from the freezer and sets it into the oven and I stare at him, wondering if there's anything this man can't do.

We eat dessert, and eventually, Libby falls asleep with Boo's head on her feet, and Butter lying on the floor beside her. When I try to nudge her awake, she grumbles and goes right back to sleep. With a sigh, I reluctantly say to Frank, "I really should wake her up and take her home. She's going to be a nightmare tomorrow if we stay much later."

Frank pushes back the curtain covering the front window and peers out at the fresh sleet falling—each drop illuminated by the lights of the porch—and frowns.

"You should stay," Frank signs.

"What?" I ask, not quite sure I understand.

Frank texts: «You should stay. It's sleeting outside and the road can get really icy.»

"Oh, I'll be fine. I have four-wheel-drive."

«You don't know the roads out here. It can be hard to see the icy spots.»

"But, we've already imposed on you enough for one day," I counter.

«I've told you, having you here hasn't been an imposition. It's been nice.»

«Besides, you've had wine.»

The wine had been drunk long enough ago now that it's probably fine, but Frank seems insistent. I gaze out the window, considering.

«I'd like you to stay.»

I read the message and my stomach flutters. When my eyes meet Frank's, he quickly snaps his gaze away.

"You would?" I ask.

Frank's ears grow red and he nearly drops his phone before texting again.

«Yeah. So I don't have to go outside in this weather to rescue you when your car skids into a ditch.»

«Also, I make really good pancakes.»

"You're sure you don't mind?"

«Of course I don't mind. I wouldn't have asked if I did.»

"Alright, fine," I concede. "But only because I can't make pancakes at my own house because of my mouse-infested, non-working stove." My shoulders slump at the thought.

Frank chuckles silently, then leads the way as I scoop Libby into my arms and carry her to the guest bedroom. There's a double bed with a wooden headboard and a fluffy, white duvet. A red and black checked blanket is folded at the foot of the bed and I pull it over her. I don't notice Frank has disappeared until he returns, a cup of water in hand. He turns on a night light and sets the cup on the bedside table before leaving again.

Several minutes later, I emerge from the bedroom feeling exhausted, but content. I flop onto the couch next to Frank, and let out a deep sigh.

"All settled in," I say quietly.

"You look tired," Frank signs. "You should go to bed too."

I glance at my watch. "It's too early," I say, a little disappointed.

We sit in silence for a moment before Frank stands and goes to the kitchen. From a high cabinet, he pulls out a bottle of whiskey and raises a questioning eyebrow at me. I nod, and he moves around the kitchen for a minute, returning with two identical glasses, each with a healthy pour of whiskey and two ice cubes. My fingers brush against his as I take one.

We clink glasses and sip, and I feel the burn of liquor in my throat as I swallow, my cheeks warming instantly. I lean my head back on the couch and let my eyes fall closed.

"This has been such a perfect day," I say quietly to Frank, not opening my eyes. "Thank you."

Frank's quiet for a long time, long enough that I crack my eyes open in time to see him sitting straight-backed on the couch, staring at me. The look is something I can't interpret, something like longing maybe? But before I can pinpoint it, Frank snaps his eyes away, standing abruptly to check the fire that's nearly burned itself out.

CHAPTER 7

FRANK

Placing a log into the fireplace, I move it around with a poker without any real purpose. I'm stalling, embarrassed that I'd once again been caught staring at Bennett, probably with a look of wanting on my face. Because there's no denying it, I *want* him. And judging by his playful little smirks every time he catches me, he probably knows it.

Long ago, I'd shut the door on all hopes of love for myself so thoroughly that allowing myself to want Bennett feels like the first day of spring after a long, cold winter. It's been so long since I've allowed myself to desire anyone, I don't know what to do or how to act.

So, I finish stoking the fire, check the weather outside again, and refill the dogs' water bowls. I'm bending down to smooth out a fold in the rug when Bennett calls my name.

"Frank," he says tiredly, head still resting on the back of the couch, "come sit down."

I do, but as tired as I'd been a few minutes ago, now I'm full of nervous energy—too hot and too wound up to rest. Pushing up the sleeves of my sweater, I lift my glass of whiskey, and take a too-big drink, the burn in my throat causing me to splutter and cough.

"You okay?" Bennett sits up and pats me on the back like he's burping a baby.

I nod, then cough again. Well, I can add humiliation to the pile of all the things I'm feeling at the moment.

"What's going on?" he asks. I lean back on the couch, coughing once more for good measure.

I try to come up with something that isn't a lie, but that isn't *I want you and I don't know what to do about it.*

I finally text: «I'm not used to having guests.»

"Oh. Well, we can go if—"

Shaking my head vigorously, I put up a hand, cutting him off.

«No, I don't want you to go. I'm just on edge, I guess.»

«I don't spend much time around other people. I forgot how to act like a normal human being.»

Bennett laughs warmly. "How about we just talk, okay?"

Relieved, I nod. And so we do.

It takes some coaxing to get me to open up and give Bennett more than a few words, but eventually I do. I tell him all about my woodworking, about some of the oddest jobs I've been called to do as a handyman—including extracting a live bear from a dumpster, twice—about how I bought the house when it had been ready to fall down, and I'd fixed it up, bit by bit.

Bennett pays attention, never talking while I'm composing a text, and never accepting a one-word answer. I've haven't told anyone as much about myself as I'm telling Bennett tonight. I've haven't ever met anyone who wants to know so much about me. The more we talk, the more I find myself wanting to say, which is new and kind of liberating. It's like some invisible bands around my chest are slowly releasing and I feel more free than I have in a long, long time.

Bennett opens his mouth to speak, then hesitates.

"What?" I sign.

"Well...I don't know if I should ask this."

"Go ahead." My heart is pounding as I wait for the question.

"Okay," Bennett says hesitantly. "But you don't have to answer if you don't want to, or if it's too sensitive of a topic."

I hold my breath, bracing myself. I'm pretty sure I know what I'm about to be asked, but not sure I'm ready to answer.

"Where is your family?"

The question takes me by surprise, leaving me open-mouthed.

"I'm sorry," Bennett says quickly. "It's too personal. Forget I asked."

«No, it's okay. It wasn't the question I expected, that's all.»

I stand, holding up a finger in the universal *just a moment* gesture. I take both empty glasses to the kitchen, coming back half a minute later with drinks refilled. Sitting down, I take a sip, then start texting again.

«My dad retired a few years after I came back to Cherry Tree. He went along with me on jobs to make sure I knew what I was doing, but after a year, he let me handle things on my own. Once I was able to run things myself, he and Mom moved to Texas.»

«Dad died a couple years after they moved, and Mom stayed with her family. All of my relatives live in Texas, so I don't have anyone here.»

I glance up to see the look of pity in Bennett's eyes. *Fuck.* I hate pity. I want this conversation to move along so I don't have to think about Dad, or how much I've been missing him lately.

Dad loved the holidays. Every year on Thanksgiving, I'd watch the parade with Mom immediately followed by the Lions game. When that was over, Dad would haul out the box of lights, drag the ladder out of the garage, and start decorating the house. My job was to untangle strands of lights and hold the ladder steady while he worked. Mom would cook while we were outside.

Once the lights were up, we'd eat dinner. Afterward, he'd gather us outside to watch as our house lit up like it belonged on the Las Vegas Strip. He'd put on a mariachi Christmas album and dance with my mom right there in the front yard. As a kid, I loved it. As a sulky teen who wanted nothing more than to be as normal as possible, it was mortifying. But now, I'd give anything to have one more Thanksgiving with him. Over the years, I've thought about putting up lights on my own house, but it doesn't feel the same to do it all by myself. So instead, I treat the day like any other, and try to block out the memories.

Dad would hate knowing I don't do anything on Thanksgiving except watch a little football, but even that makes me miss him too much. I'd like to think that if he saw me tonight, he'd be happy to see me celebrating the day with friends in my home.

I rub my eyes with the back of my hand, hoping Bennett doesn't notice.

«I text with Mom. She doesn't text back much because she has arthritis and it's hard for her, but she video calls me sometimes. She does all the talking, of course. She only learned very basic ASL, so I mostly listen. She only asks questions that I can answer yes or no to.»

«She's happy there, and I'm glad she has the family around her.»

"Are you close with the rest of your family?"

«Not really. They don't know what to say to me, or how to treat me. They say hi, but that's about it.»

"Do you think you'd ever want to move there to be closer with them?"

I don't have to think about it long before I reply.

«No. Michigan is my home. I can't imagine living anywhere else.»

"That's beautiful. And to be honest, that's a big part of why I moved here with Libby. I want her to have a sense of home."

Before I can ask more about that, Bennett moves on to another question.

"So, you said if we hadn't come over, you'd have probably spent the day watching bad movies…" I nod. "What movies would you be watching if we weren't here?"

I shake my head and duck my chin.

"And no lying," Bennett says.

«Okay, but no judgment. You promise?»

"I promise."

«Any or all of the Legally Blonde movies. Anything with Sandra Bullock. The Great British Bake Off or a Hallmark movie, if I'm feeling really wild.»

Bennett's brows shoot up in surprise. "Frank!"

«You promised you wouldn't judge.»

"I'm not! It's just...so unexpected." I look away, covering my face with my hands. "Come on." Bennett tugs my sleeve. "I think it's sweet."

«I like what I like, okay?»

"Okay, fine. But for the record, I like all of those too."

I shake my head. *He's just being nice.*

"Next time you're watching any of those movies, call me and I'll come over and watch with you. Got it?"

I laugh at the absurdity of it. I know it's not that simple, especially with Bennett being a single parent. But I play along anyway and nod.

"Great! It's a date."

Date. The word makes me feel like I'm vibrating out of my skin. I need to change the subject. Fast.

«Enough about me. What about you?»

"What about me?"

There's so much I want to know about Bennett: his favorite place to visit, his biggest fear, favorite ice cream flavor, proudest moment, hopes and dreams. I want to know about his past, and what made him who he is now.

«I want to know anything you want to tell me.»

Bennett raises his eyebrows when he reads the message. "Anything, huh?" He sips his whiskey and closes his eyes like he's deep in thought. I wait, wondering at one point if he'd fallen asleep.

A log in the fire pops, sending sparks upward and momentarily waking the dogs. Butter huffs and rolls over, kicking Boo in the head. Boo sighs and goes back to sleep.

When Bennett finally opens his eyes, he speaks softly, staring at the ceiling.

"I was married for four years. His name's Chase—fitting since he was always chasing the next thing that caught his attention." His voice doesn't sound bitter, just resigned.

"We were living in Ann Arbor when we met and we moved to New York shortly after. Things were mostly good. We got married on a whim, probably too fast, and then he became...different. Maybe I did too, I don't know. I'd told him from the beginning that I wanted a child. He always said he wanted whatever I wanted, which should've been a sign. I pushed ahead with the whole process thinking that if I kept moving forward, he'd be there too. And he was, for a while. When our friend, Sonja, agreed to be our surrogate, Chase said he wanted me to be the donor since I'm the one who wanted a child in the first place. That *really* should've tipped me off that he wasn't fully on board, but I wanted a child so badly, I ignored the red flags. When Sonja told us she was pregnant, things really started to fall apart with Chase.

"He became distant, spent more time at work, more time with friends—*his* friends, not *our* friends—and seemed to be so over all of the domestic stuff. Anything that had to do with the baby became such a chore for him. When Libby was born, Chase became so irritated that he suddenly had responsibilities that kept him from going out to dinner every night or going out with friends.

"Chase loved her, and he tried to be a good father, he really did. But as time went on, the responsibilities we shared became more and more *my* responsibilities. And Libby became *my* child instead of ours. We eventually separated, and I got a place for Libby and me. Once we moved out, Chase became less interested in Libby, and fell back into his old life. He pulled away until he was nothing more to her than a distant relative.

"So, when my mom told me she was going to sell the house here, since it had been mostly empty for the last two years, I figured this was a good time to get out of the city and start fresh with Libby. And here we are."

Bennett makes a *ta-da* gesture with his hands. As I watch him, I try to imagine how hard it must be to carry the weight of raising a child alone, especially when that child needs extra support.

I raise my glass for a toast, and Bennett clinks it with his own. After a sip, I drape an elbow on the back of the couch, letting my head rest on my bicep. My heart hurts for Bennett, who'd tried so hard to make a life and a family with someone who couldn't be bothered. It hurts that Bennett's love had been treated like a tissue: used, then thrown away. And it hurts for Libby, who's so sweet and innocent. She deserves parents who love and care for her, who make her the center of their world. She has Bennett, and as far as I can tell, he's an amazing father, so maybe that's enough for her. But he deserves someone to share parenthood with, to share his life with, to love.

«I'm sorry things didn't work out with Chase.»

"Don't be," Bennett says, running a hand over his chin. "I didn't belong there. In New York, with Chase..."

«And now?»

"Well, I'm not sure I'm cut out for outdoor life," he says, chuckling. "But I'm pretty sure *this* is where I'm supposed to be. I can feel it."

The air between us dances and hums. I roll my half-full glass between my palms before taking another sip, then setting it on the table.

"I'm glad you're here," I sign. And while I mean here in Cherry Tree, I also mean here in my home.

This. This is what it means to feel like part of a family, to *really* feel like you belong with someone else. I have to look away, swallowing hard to keep my emotions from spilling out.

"Me too," he signs back, and for the first time, he doesn't say it out loud as well. Setting his glass on the table, Bennett sighs heavily. He rests his head on the back of the couch, letting it roll to the side to face me. His face is relaxed, mouth tipped up in a small, contented smile. He lifts his hand, then holds it out in the space between us, palm up.

I regard Bennett's outstretched hand. Is this an invitation for a handshake, a *gimme five* gesture, or something else? Unsure what to do, I attempt something like a handshake. But when I place my palm into Bennett's, long fingers wrap around my own, and hold on gently, but confidently. He relaxes, closing his eyes and letting our joined hands rest on the couch.

The simplicity of the touch makes my heart thunder in my chest, and my vision goes starry at the edges. I don't know what this means. Maybe it means nothing. *But maybe it means something.*

For the first time in a long time, I hate not being able to speak out loud. If I were able to speak, I might try to make a joke, or say something, anything, to break the silence. But I can't, and anything I want to say, I'd either have to type or sign, and both options mean breaking contact.

Warm from the drink and the fire, and happy with how perfect the day has been, I have the sudden urge to lay my head on Bennett's chest. I wonder if his heartbeat is slow and relaxed, as if he's about to fall asleep, or is it pounding wildly, like mine? I wonder what he smells like. I wonder what it would be like to kiss him. Would it be sweet or commanding? Restrained or determined? Clumsy or graceful?

Perhaps it's the whiskey, or perhaps I'm just tired, but I decide to quit overthinking. On a large exhale, I relax, releasing the tension from my shoulders all the way to my fingers. My heart gradually slows down, and the jitters I'd been feeling all day fade away at last.

We stay like this for several minutes, listening to the crackles and hisses of the fire, and the soft snores of the dogs. I nearly doze off when Bennett finally speaks.

"Hey, Frank?"

I blink my eyes open and glance at him, then back to our still joined hands. Bennett pulls his hand away slowly, adjusting his body so it's angled toward me. At the loss of connection, I instantly miss the warmth of his touch.

"Earlier, when I said I wanted to ask you a personal question…"

I nod, jitters bubbling up in my chest.

"What did you think I was going to ask you?"

My eyebrows pull together tightly and I frown. For a brief moment, I consider lying, but all evening, I've found myself wanting to tell Bennett every truth I have to give. I chew on my lower lip and stare at my phone for a long moment before typing.

«I thought you were going to ask me if I'm gay.»

"Oh!" Bennett blinks a few times and looks away, flustered. "I, uh, I wouldn't. It's not my business. I mean, you *could* tell me…if you want. And if not, that's okay too."

I watch Bennett with amusement, smiling a little, despite myself. Seeing him get so discombobulated is oddly charming.

«Or, I thought you might ask why I can't speak. I was expecting one of those two questions.»

Bennett regains his composure. "Do you get those questions a lot?" he asks cautiously.

«No.»

«Yes.»

«Well, never the first question. No one's ever asked me that. But the second one, yes.»

He considers this for a moment, then asks, "Would you like me to ask you either of those questions?"

I'm touched that he doesn't just come out and ask, but rather lets me decide if I want to answer. I'm torn, not positive that I want to answer either question, but feeling like it might be a relief to talk about it.

«Honestly, I'm not sure.»

"Well," he says slowly. "How about you tell me…when you're ready, of course. It could be tonight, or next week, or never."

I think about it, then nod.

In perfect synchronicity, we both sip our drinks, then lay our heads on the back of the couch. I'm flooded with warmth—from the fire, from the whiskey, and from Bennett. I can't remember when I'd spent so much time with another person. And I don't think I've ever enjoyed being around someone as much as I do right now.

After a long, comfortable silence, I pick up my phone. I'd been so perfectly relaxed, I think I might've dozed off for a few seconds. But I suddenly have the overwhelming sense that *this* is the right moment. I need to say it.

«I'm gay.»

My heart pounds in my chest as I wait for Bennett to notice I've sent the message. I could've signed it, but I'm scared—of what, I'm not sure. My stomach is in knots, and my leg bounces unintentionally. I bite my lower lip as I wait.

Bennett's phone buzzes, and he slowly stirs, lifting his phone. He stares at the message far longer than I think it should take to read those two little words. Forcing myself to take deep breaths, I send a second text.

«I've never told anyone before.»

Finally, Bennett sits up straighter, perhaps understanding the weight of what I've just told him. Turning his whole body toward me, he asks, "No one knows?"

I shake my head. I think perhaps Evelyn suspects it, but she's never said anything to me outright. Staring into Bennett's kind eyes, the feeling of vulnerability so strong, I think I might cry on the spot. I fight the urge to pull a blanket over my head to hide my face.

"Are you worried about how people will react?" he asks.

I blow out a long breath as I think about my answer.

«I don't think so. People here are pretty nice, and I think most of them would accept me if they knew.»

Bennett waits patiently while I tap on my phone, then delete, then try again.

«I don't talk about anything personal with anyone, and no one's asked so…»

«Also, I haven't had anyone who I felt I could talk to about it. Someone I could trust who would understand.»

Bennett waits until it's clear I'm not going to type anything more. He squeezes my hand.

"Thank you for telling me," he whispers. "For the record, you can trust me, and I do understand. Coming out can be scary and overwhelming. Having someone to talk to who's gone through it can be really helpful. I'm happy to be that person for you, if that's what you want."

And then, for one brief moment, probably only the span of a blink, I catch Bennett's eyes as they flick down to my mouth and back up again. That darting glance hits me like a tidal wave, leaving me flailing in its wake.

Of course, Butter chooses *this* moment to wake from a deep sleep and snap her body to attention, tearing toward the back door and barking wildly. I hurry to the sliding glass door, push back the curtain and scan the porch, trying to hush her. I finally see what she's barking at: a couple of fat raccoons who routinely check the porch for any stray scraps of food. I suspect the raccoons also enjoy taunting Butter, because they take every opportunity to peer through the sliding glass door and stare while she loses it on the other side.

The raccoons are probably drawn to the scent of Thanksgiving dinner still hanging heavy in the air. Finding no scraps, they bumble their way back down the steps in no hurry whatsoever as I squat down, quieting Butter.

"I should probably check on Libby," Bennett says, rising from the couch. "She probably didn't hear it, but just in case."

I nod, scratching Butter behind the ears before standing. Bennett yawns and stretches his arms overhead, and I have to force myself to look away from the strip of exposed bare skin just below his shirt.

"You should go to bed," I sign.

"Yeah, okay," he says.

"You can take my bed and I'll take the couch."

Bennett shakes his head. "Oh, no. I can't let you do that. I've put you out far too much already. I'll share with Libby."

We spend the next couple of minutes going back and forth, but I eventually convince him to take my bed, assuring him that if Libby wakes up in the night, he'd be able to hear her from across the hall. I'd already changed the sheets while Bennett was putting Libby to bed anyway.

I grab some clothes for myself, and set out a pair of sweats and a t-shirt for Bennett. My heart thunders as we linger in the hallway, the air between us crackling with electricity.

"Well," Bennett says, stepping close, "goodnight, Frank. Thanks for today."

I hold my breath as he leans in and brushes a light kiss to my cheek. It's nothing but a featherlight peck, but I know that if I turn my face toward Bennett's, if I reach out to him, I'd receive a real kiss. I want it—*god, I want it so much*—but the longer we stand here, the more I let myself overthink.

What if Bennett doesn't want it? Does Bennett even like me like that? What if I'm a bad kisser?

A small noise—maybe a cough or a snore—comes from the guest bedroom where Libby is asleep. It's enough to snap me back to the present. I sign "goodnight" quickly, then hurry past Bennett, leaving him alone in the hall.

Once I'm sure he's gone into the bedroom for the night, I change clothes, brush my teeth, pull a blanket from the back of the leather armchair, and lie on the couch.

Sleep doesn't come easy. My mind keeps going back to my conversation with Bennett, to our joined hands, to the way he'd looked at me in the hallway. Today has been the best day I've had in, well, ever—and I know I'll never forget it.

CHAPTER 8

BENNETT

I stir awake, squinting as a streak of light falls across my face followed by someone—or something—licking my hand. Startled, I sit bolt upright and peer down with sleepy eyes at Boo, who's staring at me, head cocked to one side.

It takes me a few confused seconds before I discern where I am. In the light of morning, I look around Frank's bedroom, taking everything in. The bed is huge with a headboard and footboard made of dark wood accented by a gnarled edge across the top, the piece designed to accentuate the knots and imperfections in the wood—clearly custom-made by Frank. Along one wall, the built-in shelves are crowded with books and dotted with a few knick knacks, including several hand-carved wooden animals in various shapes and sizes. A leather chair, identical to the one in the living room, sits in the corner with a blanket draped over it like it's waiting for someone to sink in and be embraced by it.

The decor of the room is similar to the rest of the house: rustic, practical, and cozy, like a vacation cabin in the mountains. Every part of it makes me want to wrap myself in a soft blanket, curl my hands around a steaming mug of coffee, and stay in bed all day, preferably next to someone I love.

I swing my tired legs out of bed and shuffle my way down the hall to check on Libby. I expect to see Frank asleep on the couch, and Libby in the guest bedroom playing on her iPad. Instead, I find her sitting on her knees in a chair at the kitchen island, and Frank standing on the other side facing her, the two of them engaged in some kind of conversation. I stay in the shadow of the hallway, watching the two of them chatting with their hands.

Libby, full of smiles, makes a fist and taps it twice on the palm of her other hand—the sign for 'knock knock.' Frank signs 'who's there?,' but Libby doesn't answer. She makes the gesture again, and again, Frank signs his response, even more exaggerated this time, Libby laughing in response. Then, Frank makes a knocking sound on the countertop of the island. Libby looks around, intentionally not hearing the knock. He does it again, and this time, she puts a hand to her ear, as if trying to hear better. She falls into giggles and Frank soundlessly laughs along with her.

"Are the two of you telling knock-knock jokes?" I ask, fully making my way into the kitchen.

I smile to myself, noticing how Frank's eyes quickly rake over me—wearing the borrowed sweatpants and t-shirt—before signing "good morning."

He turns his attention back to the stove, where he pours a cup of batter onto a hot pan, a flush creeping down the back of his neck. I pad barefoot to the chair where Libby is kneeling and I hug her, lifting her off the chair easily.

"How long have you been up?" I ask. She shrugs.

"A while," Frank signs. "Libby is an early bird."

"Believe me, I know. I'm sorry if she woke you up."

"She didn't," he responds. "The dogs did."

I have a feeling he's lying to spare me the guilt.

A pot of coffee sits on the corner of the island—its strong, intoxicating scent too enticing for me to ignore. Helping myself to a mug, I ask, "Why didn't you wake me up?"

Frank shakes his head. "You're a single parent. I thought you could use the extra sleep."

I'm not sure why, but that statement, probably intended to be light, makes me feel seen for the first time in too long. I nearly burst into tears at his thoughtfulness.

"You can go lie down again, if you want," he signs. "Get some more rest."

"No, I'm good. Even though it's only—" I glance at the clock, "—eight-seventeen, I've gotten more sleep than I have in a long time."

He nods, flipping the pancake on the cast iron griddle, a perfect sizzling sound emanating as it makes contact with the heat. Minutes later, he sets a plate each of perfectly cooked pancakes in front of Libby and me at the dining table, his movements a little stiff and awkward.

I'd been so hungry that it's not until I'm halfway through my breakfast that I notice Frank has disappeared. He'd been at the stove finishing the pancakes, but he's not there anymore. Libby is engrossed in her own breakfast, hands sticky with syrup, so I figure she hasn't noticed he's gone either.

I'm rinsing my plate in the sink when Frank reappears wearing his usual worn jeans and soft-looking hoodie with a faded Wayne State University logo on the front.

"Going somewhere?" I ask, mostly joking. He nods once, eyes focused on the countertop.

«Got a couple of people that need help this morning.»

«Feel free to stay as long as you like. Leave the dishes and close the door behind you when you go. The door locks on its own.»

I stare at him in silence. *Are there actual emergencies? Or is he uncomfortable and trying to escape?* I know I didn't imagine the magnetic pull toward each other last night. I saw the joy on Frank's face this morning. *So what happened?*

I watch closely as Frank pulls on a beanie and tugs on his boots. As he's shrugging into his coat, his gaze catches on mine. His eyes look heavy and tired, and there's a deep crease between his eyebrows.

Looking away, he takes a set of keys off the hook and stuffs them into his pocket.

"Frank?" I keep my voice soft as I approach the doorway. "Are you... are *we* okay?"

His eyes meet mine, and a tiny sliver of tension eases from his face and shoulders.

"Yes," he signs.

I reach out a hand to him. He takes it without hesitation and I squeeze, feeling rough calluses and heat.

"I want you to know," I say, not letting go of his hand, "I had an amazing day yesterday, and last night was really special to me. I love getting to know you."

He nods slowly.

"And," I say, making sure he's looking at me, "Everything you told me last night? I promise to keep it between us."

I release his hand, and he signs "thank you." I give him one last look—one that I hope conveys my sincerity—before heading back into the kitchen. Frank gives Libby a fist bump and leaves without another word.

As I clear plates and gather mine and Libby's things, I wonder about Frank's shift in mood, going from easy laughter with Libby to awkward and uncomfortable as soon as I showed up. I don't understand, especially when he seemed so comfortable last night. I hope our almost-kiss before bed didn't put him off. But, no. I saw the look in his eyes, and the way he'd been looking at me all day. There was no denying there was *something* happening between us. Maybe it had to do with coming out to me? He said he hadn't told anyone else, so maybe he was feeling some kind of way about it?

On the drive home, I get a text.

Frank: «I meant to say thank you for yesterday. You were so incredibly generous to include me in your holiday.»

I wait until I'm home to respond.

Bennett: Not at all! I owe you a thousand thank yous for opening your home to us. It meant the world to me to give Libby such a special holiday.

Frank: «You're always welcome.»

I'm not sure that's true after the way he'd left so abruptly this morning.

Bennett: I hope we didn't overstay our welcome. I didn't mean to run you out of your own home.

Frank: «You didn't. It was me.»

Bennett: Meaning...?

It's several minutes before Frank responds.

Frank: «I needed to clear my head. Nothing bad, just had to think about things.»

Bennett: Frank, please talk to me if anything is bothering you. Okay?

Frank: «I will. And thanks for listening last night.»

Bennett: Anytime.

For the next two weeks, I don't see much of Frank. We text a little, and he tells me at least half a dozen times that he wants to get together. But he says December is a frenzy of work in his workshop and various people need help with holiday-related tasks. When I ask what "holiday-related tasks" means, he gives me a short list of things he's been doing since we last saw each other: helping put up the official Cherry Tree

Christmas tree, hanging lights and decorations throughout downtown, dropping off bags of ice-melt at various homes of elderly townspeople, and the list goes on. Frank says that by the time he's done helping people, he still has to spend hours in the workshop finishing custom gifts that had been ordered for Christmas.

I suggest grabbing a coffee or a beer, but Frank declines the first, saying he has too many errands to run, and the second because he's too exhausted at the end of the day. On Thursday, I nearly collide with him as he's coming out of the Cherry Tree Café. He has a cup in one hand and a box of pastries in the other. Frank is so harried, he does a double take before recognizing me.

"Hi," I say, grinning. Frank gives me a small smile. "How've you been?"

Too late, I recognize that his hands are full, leaving him unable to type or sign. Taking the box and coffee from his hands, I wait while he types on his phone.

«Good. Busy with the holidays.»

I wait for more, but Frank doesn't elaborate. I take in his appearance: hair haphazardly stuffed under a baseball cap, flannel shirt speckled with sawdust and paint, and dark circles under his weary eyes. It's like his whole body is radiating stress.

"Are you in a hurry right now?" I ask, though it's clear he is.

"A little bit," Frank signs.

"Well, before you go," I say, talking quickly, "I heard about a holiday festival in Traverse City that sounds like fun. I thought maybe you could come on Saturday with Libby and me."

«Already going.»

"Oh. Okay." My face falls and my cheeks burn. Frank frowns, then types again.

«I'm sorry. This time of year is rough for me.»

When I look up at him, his face has softened, and he genuinely seems to mean it.

"I understand. No problem." I swallow thickly.

«I'm helping a couple people with their booths at the festival, so I have to go early.»

«I'll be there all day. I don't know where I'll be, but tell me when you get there and we'll meet up, okay?»

"Sounds great," I say, trying not to sound too eager. Frank gives me a tired smile as I hand him back his coffee and pastry box. "See you soon," I say.

He gives me an awkward nod before hurrying off.

A warm snap brings mild weather to the holiday festival, which means that the outdoor event is crowded with locals and tourists alike. It's late afternoon, busy enough that I have to park a few blocks away. I text Frank to let him know we've arrived, then take Libby's hand as we head toward the festival.

The scents of fall fill the air—apples and cinnamon, chestnuts and pine. Libby and I meander through the crowd, browsing the various booths. We buy giant soft pretzels, warm cider, and a bag of fresh kettle corn. At a booth selling stuffed animal toys, I pick out a fuzzy, handmade dog wearing a moss-green sweater. I tell myself it's because Libby loves dogs and not because the dog's sweater reminds me of the one Frank wore on Thanksgiving. All the while I keep an eye out for Frank who, so far, is nowhere to be seen.

Libby insists on playing every carnival game we encounter, although I draw the line at the win-a-goldfish game. I know I'd be the one to end up taking care of it, and I don't need that right now. While she's perusing a booth full of handmade toys, I send another text to Frank, who I haven't heard from since arriving. I try not to be disappointed, telling myself he's here because he has a job to do. A little flicker of doubt creeps in and I wonder if maybe he doesn't want to see me. Maybe we haven't seen each other lately because he simply doesn't want to.

Passing a booth that's painted to look like a log cabin, the scent of sugar and fried dough of the apple cider doughnuts is too tempting to pass up. I end up buying half a dozen—warm and fresh out of the fryer—and sharing the first one with Libby. The sweet, sticky sugar clings to our lips and fingers as we eat, but the doughnuts are heavenly.

The string lights over the street glow warmly as the sun sets and the sky turns an inky dark blue. We've been here for more than three hours when Libby signs, "I'm tired." She drags her feet as she signs, "Can we go home?"

It's close to her bedtime and I know I should get her home soon if I want to avoid a grumpy child tomorrow. I still haven't found Frank, but I can't keep Libby up late just so I can look for someone who may or may not still be here. *And who may or may not want to see me.*

Hands full of snacks, trinkets, and the little stuffed dog, I stop to readjust, and to check one last time for a text from Frank. Still no response. My heart sinks as I put my phone back in my pocket. By the time I'm ready again, I find myself surrounded by a large group of teens talking loudly and moving slowly. I have to dodge and weave my way to the other side, but once the group passes, Libby is nowhere to be seen.

My heart hammers in my chest and panic immediately sets in. I whip my head around, eyes scanning every person around me. Nothing.

"Libby!" I shout, knowing it's in vain. She hadn't worn her hearing aids tonight—typical for events like this, as she said they only make noises louder and voices more garbled—so it would be nearly impossible to hear me calling her name. But that doesn't stop me from doing it anyway.

I search frantically, not knowing in which direction to go. I look at every person and every booth, but still no sign of her. A cold sweat gathers on my face and hands. When I reach the metal barricades at the edge of the festival, I drop everything on the ground and pull out my phone to call Frank.

CHAPTER 9

FRANK

I am utterly exhausted. My muscles ache and my body is dragging after staying up past midnight putting up festival decorations and waking early to help set up booths this morning. All day, my phone has been buzzing relentlessly with calls and texts asking me to pick up something from here and take it there, find that person and give them this, help this person carry those boxes to that booth, and on and on. It's early evening, I'm ready to collapse.

The only thing I want to do is to find Bennett and Libby, take them to get fresh cider doughnuts, and go home.

There'd been a text earlier from Bennett saying he and Libby had arrived, but I got pulled away to help someone else before I had a chance to respond. I've been keeping an eye out for the two of them, but I haven't seen them yet. The mild weather means that the crowds are so dense that it's hard to locate anyone in the sea of faces.

It's after eight when I'm finally able to take a break. Ducking behind a row of booths, I sit on the curb and check my phone. Before I can look through my texts, my phone vibrates with a call. Bennett.

"Hello? Frank?" Bennett's voice doesn't have its usual friendly tone, or even the frenzied voice he uses when something is broken that needs fixing. It's shaky and desperate.

"I'm here at the festival, and I've lost Libby. We were getting ready to leave, and I stopped for a few seconds. I thought she stopped too, but I guess she didn't. When I looked up, she was gone."

«Where did you see her last?»

I listen but I'm already up and walking quickly. I'm not sure where I'm going, I just know I need to start looking.

"We were by the big gingerbread house. The one with the cutouts that you stick your head through to take pictures. She was tired, and we were heading toward the car, but I don't know if she left the festival or not."

«Check the exit where you came in. Maybe she went that way.»

«She wouldn't leave the festival without you, would she?»

"No, I don't think so. But I'll check the exit. Maybe someone saw her."

«If you see a security guard, ask them to call around. I'll keep looking around the area inside the festival.»

"Okay. Thanks, Frank."

«We'll find her.»

I disconnect the call and run toward the gingerbread house. Scouring the rows of booths, I narrowly avoid clumps of people meandering slowly through the streets.

While I'm not a parent myself, the panic I feel is real, and the thought of anything happening to Libby makes my guts clench with fear. Passing booth after booth, I search, determined to find her.

As I jog past the information tent, a familiar sound stops me in my tracks. The loud trill of a whistle *breeeeps* in a flurry of long and short tweets. I glance around for the source, my eyes landing on the familiar face of a little girl with wide eyes and a silver whistle in her mouth.

Beside her are two security guards, a short woman with copper skin and black hair, and a tall white man with a buzz cut, angular and shrewd. The woman has a hand on Libby's wrist to keep her from running away, but holding her this way means that Libby doesn't have her hands free to sign. The moment Libby's eyes meet mine, she wriggles and flails to free herself from the grip of the security guard, who shouts at her to stop.

I reach for my phone to text Bennett, but Libby races toward me and launches herself into my arms as soon as she's within catching distance. I nearly burst into tears with happiness, picking her up and hugging her tightly. I pat her gently on the back to soothe her. The security guards surround the two of us in seconds.

"Sir, is this your daughter?" the woman asks. I shake my head. Without a moment's hesitation, she speaks again, firmer this time. "Sir, if this isn't your daughter, I'm going to need you to put her down."

The second guard stands menacingly close, one hand on his hip. I try to set Libby down, but she only clings tighter. When it's clear that she isn't going to let go, the guards look at each other before the woman says, "Please follow me."

I comply, still carrying Libby, with the male guard following closely behind. I try to get my phone out of the front pocket of my jacket, but Libby is clinging tightly to my chest.

Once we reach the information tent, I kneel down, setting Libby on her feet next to me. Keeping my eyes on the female security guard, I sign "phone?" She doesn't understand the sign, so I try the more outdated sign, holding my thumb and pinky up to my face like an old-school telephone receiver.

She begrudgingly nods, and I slowly take my phone out and open the note I have saved for emergencies. In big letters, it says '**My name is Frank Garza. I can hear but can't speak. I communicate by typing or ASL.**' I always have the note ready to use so I don't have to type it out every time someone new tries to communicate with me.

Turning the phone toward the security guards, I wait while they read the message. They nod, and I type a new message.

«This is Libby Oliver. She's deaf. Her dad is Bennett Oliver.»

The guards give each other a silent look I can't interpret. The woman kneels down, addressing Libby.

"What's your name?" she asks. Libby stares, then looks at me. She can read lips on a basic level, but the way she's gripping my hand, I think she's more scared than anything.

"WHAT'S...YOUR...NAME?" the guard repeats, louder and exaggerating her mouth movements. I try not to roll my eyes. Someone needs to tell her that exaggerating her mouth as she speaks actually makes it harder to read lips. In fact, these guards could use a whole training session on how to speak with people who have communication disabilities.

I tap Libby's shoulder and sign "name."

"L-I-B-B-Y," she fingerspells to the guard, who looks to me for confirmation.

"And your dad's name is Bennett?"

I repeat the security guard's words to Libby in sign. Libby nods vigorously this time.

"You know this man?" the male security guard asks, pointing to me.

Libby steps closer to me and fingerspells "F-R-A-N-K" and then makes the sign for "friend." Both guards shrug.

Turning her attention back to me, the woman asks, "Do you have her father's number?"

I click around on my phone until I find Bennett's contact information. With shaking hands, I press 'send' and hand the phone to her, then watch as she waits for Bennett to answer.

"Hello? Bennett Oliver?" she says. "No, this is Jodie from festival security. We found your daughter... Yes. She's fine. She's here with a Frank Guzman?... Garza, right. He's... yes, he told us. Okay... The information tent on the corner of Elm and 1st... Yes, sir. Okay."

The woman, Jodie, disconnects the call and hands the phone back to me. "He's on his way."

I repeat the information to Libby in sign, and she nods, looking relieved. I stand, scooping her into my arms, holding her tightly as we wait. She puts her head on my shoulder, and I instinctively rub her back and sway side to side in an effort to comfort her. Exhaling deeply, I release some of the tension in my shoulders and back. Against my chest, I feel Libby's breaths slow, and her tiny body relaxes. My legs and back ache from working all day, but I'll gladly hold her like this for hours, as long as I can make her feel safe.

After what feels like an eternity, I hear Bennett's voice cut through the crowd of people.

"Libby?"

Bennett skids to a stop, his gaze catching on me holding his little girl. A huge, relieved smile splits across his face.

"Libby!" he cries. Her head is on my shoulder, and her face is turned toward my neck, buried under her arms, which are still wrapped around me.

I gently bounce her up and down a couple of times to get her attention, then turn so she can see Bennett. Her entire face lights up and she cries a garbled mess of syllables that sounds something like "Daddy." Bennett leans close, and I carefully place Libby into his waiting arms. As they embrace, crying into one another's shoulders, I shove my hands in my pockets and stare at the ground.

Finally, Bennett sets Libby on the ground, and she begins signing quickly, her hands a flurry of movement as she recounts the experience. At one point in her retelling, she pulls the red cord with the whistle from around her neck, showing Bennett how she managed to get my attention.

As I wait, I type a message, showing it to the two guards.

«Are we okay to go?»

"Yes," Jodie says. "Have a good night."

Not wanting to spend a single second more in the security tent, I gently squeeze Bennett's shoulder, guiding him toward the exit. Libby, holding on tightly to Bennett, reaches with her free hand and grips two of my fingers like she's afraid to let go. I venture a glance at Bennett, who catches my eye for a brief second, and smiles before turning his attention back to Libby.

We're all quiet as we make our way to the exit, the three of us holding hands. When we reach Bennett's car, I give Libby a hug, then wait, sitting on the back bumper while Bennett gets her settled into her seat. He closes the car door and approaches me, stepping close enough that his thighs brush my knees.

"Thank you, Frank," he says, a mixture of exhaustion and relief in his voice, "for helping to find Libby."

I shake my head, and sign, "I didn't find her. I just talked to the security guards. That's all."

"Stop." Bennett's voice has an exasperated edge to it. "Stop being so...so unwilling to accept a thank you, okay?" I stare in surprise. "Yeah, I would've found her eventually, but she was scared and lost and couldn't communicate with the security guards. You calmed her down, you talked to the guards, and you called me. Not to mention, the whole reason she was able to get your attention was because of the whistle *you* gave her."

A knot forms in my stomach thinking about how scared Libby had looked when I saw her, blowing frantically on her whistle to catch my attention.

"I'm sorry," I sign. "I'm not good at..."

People is what I want to say. I don't have conversations like this. Ever. Normally, when someone thanks me, I nod, accept whatever is offered to me, and walk away. But this is different. I hadn't fixed Bennett's washing machine or patched a hole in his roof. When I try to come up with a response, I'm at a loss for words. *Fitting*, I think.

"Listen," Bennett says. "I need to get Libby home and put her to bed. I know you must be exhausted, but..." I watch as Bennett rakes his fingers through his tousled hair. "Would you come over?"

My eyebrows pull together in confusion, and I point to myself, as if to say, "Me?"

"No, that other guy standing next to you," Bennett says as he rolls his eyes. "Of course *you!*"

Heat rises in my cheeks. "When?"

"It'll take a little while to get home and get Libby to sleep, but... forty-five minutes?"

As much as I want to go my house, crash in bed, and sleep for the next twelve hours, my desire to do anything Bennett asks is stronger.

I nod, then text:

«I need to grab my things and go home to let the dogs out.»

«An hour?»

"Perfect."

Bennett pulls his keys from his pocket, a small smile spreading across his lips. He opens the door and slides into the driver's seat. "See you soon."

I nod and Bennett winks before driving away.

Boo and Butter dance excitedly around my feet the instant I walk in the door. I let them wander around outside while I brush my teeth and pull a fresh change of clothes out of the closet. Once the dogs are back in the house, I opt to take a quick shower since I'd been running around all day and don't want to smell like it. It also helps to calm my racing heart. I'm not sure what to expect when I show up at Bennett's, but I'm pretty sure I haven't been invited over to play chess.

Pulling on a thick, charcoal grey fisherman's sweater and a pair of soft, dark jeans, I run fingers through my freshly washed hair, then hurry out the door.

Normally, I drive in silence, preferring the quiet to the incessant rhythms of pop music, but tonight, I turn on the radio and drum my fingers nervously to the beat, trying to distract myself as I pass through town on the way to Bennett's house.

I take the steps of the porch two at a time and raise a hand to knock, but the door swings open before my knuckles make contact.

Bennett's still wearing the clothes he'd had on at the festival—tailored navy pants and a thin black sweater—and his hair is messy, but in more of a casual way, less disheveled. The lines on his face are softer, too, like he finally let himself unwind after the ordeal he'd been through tonight.

What strikes me most are Bennett's eyes. An hour ago, they'd been tired and scared in equal measure, wide and weary. Now, they're focused with an intensity I haven't seen before. They are wild and hungry. *For me.*

I've never been looked at like this before, never been *wanted* like this before, and the thought of Bennett looking at me this way sends a bolt of heat up my spine.

Without a word, Bennett clutches my sweater, pulling me close. I follow his lead as he steps into the house, closing the door behind us. The instant it clicks shut, Bennett splays his hands flat against my chest, making my breath hitch, and I find myself being gently pushed until my back is against the door. I have to look up to keep eye contact, my gaze never leaving Bennett's. He inches closer, until there's only a whisper of space between us.

Time halts as we stare at each other. I'm sure Bennett can feel my heart pounding wildly under my sweater, and I wonder if his is doing the same. The air we share feels charged, tingles of electricity crackling between us like lightning is about to strike. I swallow hard and watch Bennett's eyes drop to my mouth.

"Frank," Bennett whispers. "Can I—"

But before he can finish the question, I lean in and brush my lips over his, an answering whisper of my own.

CHAPTER 10

BENNETT

Frank's kiss is cautious, not really a kiss at all, but a delicate graze of lips. He pulls his head back and lets out a shaky breath. All thoughts escape my mind as I slowly drag my hands up his chest until they're resting on strong, broad shoulders.

I slide my hand around the back of Frank's neck, combing my fingers through his short, dark hair, and watch him shiver. Leaning in, I press a light kiss to his lips, and wait. Bringing a hand up between us, Frank traces a line with his thumb over my jaw, my chin, my bottom lip, almost like he's exploring.

His lips close over mine and a rush of sparks shoots through my body. Stepping closer, I press our chests together and he sighs, relaxing into my touch. When my tongue lightly sweeps over his lower lip, he shudders. Frank's every response to my touches makes me hungry for more, like I can't quite get enough.

I pause, searching Frank's face for...*what*? Signs I'm moving too fast? Signs I should keep going? Signs I should stop? I don't know.

The questions don't linger long, because this time it's Frank who pulls my face to his, the determination in his movements sending heat up my spine. Frank parts his lips, and I answer, covering his mouth with my own. Fireworks explode into a thousand lights as we move and breathe together.

Frank's kisses aren't practiced or graceful. They're the kisses of someone without a lot of experience: a little clumsy, a little shaky. But they're perfect.

Frank tips his head back, giving me access to his neck. The smell of his peppermint soap mixed with the lingering scent of sawdust on his sweater intoxicates me. I want to consume him, and to be consumed in return.

Frank breathes rapidly as I press kisses to his earlobe, working my way down to the sensitive pulse point just under his jaw. His heartbeat is strong enough that I can feel the rhythm on my lips.

"Frank," I whisper, and he responds with a gravelly moan. It's only the second time I've heard his voice and it immediately sets me on fire. *Jesus.*

With every kiss, every touch, I can hear Frank panting, can feel his shaky hands as they touch me, like he still isn't sure he's allowed to do such a thing.

"Frank," I whisper again. His strong hands grip my sweater urgently, pulling me even closer, then spinning me around and backing me up against the door. His nerves seem to have melted away, because I find myself being manhandled by Frank, and I'm not mad about it. At all.

I'm surrounded by Frank, caged in by arms, legs, body. I'm lost in his kisses, his breath, his heat. I slot a thigh between his solid legs and he answers with a roll of his hips. I've never been so thankful for a door in all my life, because the way my knees weaken, it's the only thing keeping me upright.

All at once, Frank breaks our kiss, putting a hand on my chest and stepping back. The moment is broken in an instant, snapping like a rubber band pulled too tight. I reach forward, but he takes another step back, eyes fixed on the floor.

"Frank?" I say slowly. "Are you okay?" He nods, then shakes his head like he can't make up his mind.

"I'm okay," he signs, "but..."

I watch as he furrows his brow, seeming to struggle with his thoughts. I want to help—to jump in and guess what he wants to say. But I know better. Libby always gets upset whenever someone tries to finish her sentences before she can sign whatever it is she's trying to say. So I wait.

Instead of signing more, however, Frank drags his hands over his face, suddenly looking so tired. When it seems no more words are forthcoming, I speak again, quieter this time.

"If I've misread things..." I try, "or, if I've done something wrong..."

Frank's eyes snap up, and he shakes his head, as if to say *no, no, no.*

"Then, please," I beg. "Talk to me."

I go to the couch, and Frank follows. He sits heavily and puts enough distance between himself and me that the space feels like a vast chasm. I want nothing more than to scoot closer, but he sits stiffly and stares at his shoes, so I stay put.

Something tells me I should wait for him to speak first. The clock in the hall punctuates every second that goes by. The fridge hums and somewhere outside, a dog barks. The house is cool, not nearly as cozy as Frank's. Yet, in this moment, it feels too warm.

After a minute, Frank signs, "I'm sorry."

"You don't need to apologize," I say, angling my body to face him. "You didn't do anything wrong."

He signs, "I...," before sighing and pulling out his phone.

«I'm sorry. I think we should stop.»

"Oh," I say, suddenly feeling guilty, thinking maybe I pushed him too far. "Did I do something wrong?"

«No, it wasn't anything you did.»

«I think we should just be friends.»

When I read the message, I feel like I've been kicked in the gut. My mind grapples for reasons. I look up to find Frank chewing on his bottom lip and staring nervously at me.

"Why?" I ask, trying to keep my voice neutral. "I mean, of course I'll respect your wishes. But it seemed like you were into what we were doing. It seemed like you were into...me."

Thinking about our kiss, I'm certain I could feel how much Frank liked what we'd been doing. I'd felt the desire, the attraction between us.

«I was. I am.»

«I like you a lot.»

"But you don't want...," I gesture between the two of us. "...this?"

My eyes flick to Frank, then to my phone and back again. He taps the screen, but no texts come. My phone shows three dots appearing, then disappearing, over and over, like he can't find the words he wants to say. Or maybe he's trying to let me down easy.

"Just say it!" I blurt. Frank looks up, surprised, and I immediately regret my outburst. I shouldn't have snapped, but I'm tired—we both are—and I don't understand what happened.

"I'm sorry," I say. "But if you're worried about hurting my feelings, don't. I'd rather you just tell me."

The truth is, I don't really want to know, especially if it means I can't have Frank. But those dots on the screen were taunting me. They'd made it painfully clear that he's struggling with something he doesn't want to tell me.

Finally, he starts typing quickly and sends a string of texts.

«I like you.»

«Really, really like you.»

«I enjoy being with you so much.»

«No one's ever talked with me the way you do.»

«Being around you made me realize I've never had a real friend until now.»

«You're the first.»

At first, I don't understand what he's trying to say. It's a truth, small and simple, but so, so heavy. The admission makes my heart hurt for Frank. How could anyone not want to get to know him? How could he have lived almost forty years without a close friend? I don't ask, but it probably also means that he's never had a boyfriend either.

"You don't think we could do both?" I ask. "Friends and...more?"

Frank shrugs, and his face looks pained.

«Maybe.»

«But maybe not.»

«And if things don't work out, I don't want to lose you as a friend. Going back to my life without you, and without Libby... I don't want that.»

"You wouldn't lose me. I'd be your friend no matter what."

«People say that, but it rarely works that way.»

«When people break up, they try to stay friends, but it gets too hard. The pain of watching someone you love move on...it hurts too much.»

«I'd rather have you as a friend than nothing at all.»

I gaze at Frank—his sad, tired eyes, the deep lines between his brows—and wish I could give him every assurance that things will work out. I want to argue. Not argue, but lay out all the reasons I think he's wrong. Of course I'll still be friends with him if the romance doesn't work out. *Won't I?* And why is Frank so sure it won't work out anyway?

This is Frank's way, I'm learning. He needs time and space to work through his feelings. This might all be too fast for him, and he may simply need room to think about everything. After all, he's been alone for most of his adult life. And now, here I am, invading all the spaces of his life that he isn't used to sharing...and still pushing for more.

"Are you sure this is what you want?" I ask, my throat tight.

«No. But it's what I need.»

«For now.»

I'm not sure I understand his answer, but before I can ask, he stands, pressing the heels of his hands to his eyes. He walks past me toward the door, stepping just far enough away that we don't touch.

I follow, desperate to say more, but not sure what. When he pulls the door open, a cold wind blows in from outside causing me to shiver. Frank seems impervious, his mind clearly elsewhere. I lean against the doorframe, shoving my hands in my pockets. He's just about to leave when he turns. I've never seen him look so incredibly sad.

"Are you okay to drive?" I ask, because I can't think of anything better.

He nods, then looks like he wants to say something. Instead, he turns and walks down the steps, gets into his truck, and drives away.

I press my forehead against the doorframe, breathing deeply and letting the wintry air soothe the sting in my eyes. I allow myself to feel angry and hurt for the space of three deep breaths before going back inside, shutting the door behind me.

I keep my word, respecting Frank's decision to be friends. Since our conversation after the festival, every text I think about sending is fraught with second guessing. I worry that sending a simple '*I hope you're having a good day,*' text might be interpreted as pressure for more.

It feels like a blessing that the week goes by in a blur. Each day bleeds into the next as I try to finish my work before Libby's winter break. Since being hired at the community college, I've been helping another professor with a research project that's scheduled through January. Then I'll be teaching two English classes of my own.

Libby's school is set to close for two weeks after the holiday show—a schoolwide program that includes singing, dancing, and as far as I can tell, at least half a pound of glitter attached to each student's non-religious costume—on Friday. Having her home until after New Year's means that I won't get much work done during that time. So I've cleared my schedule and plan on spending the break having some much needed father-daughter time. Unfortunately, that means doing as much work as possible until then.

I'm dropping Libby off at school on Friday morning, more than ready to finish the hectic week and start the winter break.

As we're walking into the building, Libby signs, "Is Frank coming to my holiday show tonight?" Her eyes shine with hope.

I hold back a sigh and reply, "Probably not."

Her face falls into a disappointed frown.

"Why not?"

"I didn't ask him. He's very busy right before Christmas."

"Is that why he hasn't come over?" she asks.

Well, shit. I'd been hoping she hadn't noticed we haven't spent any time with Frank since the night of the festival.

"Yes. A lot of people need his help, and he has a lot of things to make in his workshop before Christmas."

At the words *workshop* and *Christmas*, her eyes grow wide with fascination.

"Is Frank one of Santa's elves?"

I laugh at the mental image of Frank in a festive hat and pointy shoes, bent over his table, lovingly making wooden toys.

"No, he's not an elf. Come on, let's get you to class." I put a hand on her shoulder to guide her into the building, but she plants her feet, standing defiantly on the sidewalk.

"Ask him to come. Please?"

I look at my watch. If we don't get inside in the next minute or two, Libby will be marked late.

"Okay," I sign. "I'll send him a message as soon as I get back to the car. But he might not be able to come."

"But he might," Libby replies, brightening.

"Please try not to be disappointed if he doesn't show up."

"F-I-N-E," she spells, jutting her lip out in an exaggerated pout, followed by a dramatic eye roll. *God, what's she going to be like in five years, ten years?* I shudder to think.

My heart skips at the thought of messaging Frank, and possibly seeing him tonight. As much as I don't want Libby to get her hopes up, the advice had really been meant for myself. Because I know that if I ask and he declines, I'll be more disappointed than Libby.

We make it inside just in the nick of time. As promised, once I'm back in the car, I compose a text to Frank. Then I delete and start again. And again. And again. *Stop overthinking*, I tell myself. I close my texts and leave a voicemail instead.

"Hi Frank, it's Bennett. Sorry this is last minute, but Libby has a holiday show at her school tonight and she, and I, wanted to invite you. It'll be an hour of kids singing and dancing, which probably isn't your thing, but Libby has some kind of surprise she's doing in the show. She won't tell me what it is, but she's really excited. Aaaand, I think there might be cookies afterwards? But don't quote me on that. Anyway, it's at the elementary school auditorium at 6:30. We both hope you can make it, but if you can't, no big deal. Like I said, it's last minute, and you're probably really busy. Um, okay. I hope to see you. Let's not be strangers, okay? Bye, Frank."

I end the call and drop my forehead to the steering wheel of my car, taking several deep breaths before heading home.

When I pull into my driveway, I see Evelyn next door, standing on her porch, sneering at a large box that's sitting at the bottom of the steps like it's committed some horrible injustice.

"Hi, Ms. Evelyn," I call, crossing the yard to her house. "Can I help you with that?"

"Oh, Bennett! How nice to see you." She pulls her cardigan tighter around her shoulders and shivers. "That darn delivery driver dropped off this box, but he left it all the way down there. It's too heavy for me to lift."

"Want me to bring it inside for you?"

"Would you, please?"

"Of course!" I lift one corner experimentally. The box feels like it's filled with bricks. With great effort and a couple of *oofs*, I heft the box into my arms and carry it onto Evelyn's porch. She shuffles to the door, taking far too long to open it. My arms shake with fatigue as I wait for her to hold the door open for me.

"Those drivers," she complains as I lug the box inside. "I know they have a hard job to do, especially this time of year, but would it kill them to bring the box to the porch? That man was young and muscular. I think I would've enjoyed watching him bring it up here. I can't be lifting a box full of books up the stairs at my age."

"Books?" No wonder the box weighs at least fifty pounds. Evelyn points to a spot on the floor for me to place it.

"Oh, yes. I buy books for everyone on my list. I never know what to buy for anyone, but books are a pretty safe bet."

"I agree," I say with conviction. I'm about to go, but Evelyn continues to chat, putting the kettle on the stove as if we both have all the time in the world. I think about all the things I need to do today, but remember what Frank had said. *She's lonely and likes conversation.* Surely I can spare a few minutes.

As the water heats, Evelyn sits at the table and gestures for me to do the same.

"It was a blessing you came home when you did," she remarks. "I was about to call Frankie, the poor dear." At the mention of Frank's name, my heart skips.

"Frankie?"

"Oh, I'm supposed to call him Frank, aren't I? Nearly forty, that man, but I still can't bring myself to call him Frank. That was his daddy's name, you know."

"Yeah, he mentioned that."

"He's just like his father. Looks like him, acts like him, does the same job... The only difference is that Frank, the older one, could talk your ear off. My word, that man loved to tell stories."

I try to imagine it: an older version of Frank telling stories, talking animatedly, and laughing loudly. The thought makes me chuckle to myself.

"It's a shame what happened to Frankie. Used to be a little chatterbox, too. Before the..." She taps a finger to the side of her head.

"Oh?"

"Yes, the poor kid. Got a brain tumor when he was just a child. Doctors removed it, but it was in the spot that controls the muscles for speech. For a while after that, he'd make sounds, but he couldn't make words. Eventually, he just went quiet."

I'd wondered what caused Frank's disability, but he hadn't told me, and I hadn't felt comfortable asking. I assumed it was something he'd been born with. I can't imagine Frank speaking words out loud.

The kettle whistles, and Evelyn hops up, shuffling around the kitchen, placing one teabag each into two cups. I offer to help, but she waves me off.

"It must've been so hard for him and his family," I say. The thought of Frank, so young and vulnerable, going through such an ordeal makes my chest ache. I can't begin to imagine going through something like that with Libby.

"It was," Evelyn says as she pours hot water into the teacups. "He was in and out of the hospital for a year, maybe two. The town rallied around them, though. Had all kinds of fundraisers to help the Garzas out. Didn't you still live here at the time?"

I don't answer right away, racking my brain and vaguely remembering details: posters with the face of a kindergartener who'd gone to my school. I must've been in second or third grade at the time. For a few months at the end of the school year, that little kid's face—large brown eyes, dark shaggy hair, a shy smile that highlighted a missing front tooth—was everywhere. But then I'd been sent to Indiana to stay with my grandparents for the summer, and by the time I got back, I'd forgotten all about the kid on the posters. Shortly after that, my parents divorced and I moved away for good.

"That was Frank?" I ask, the pieces falling into place.

"Oh yes," she says. "Our little Frankie. After the surgery, it took him months to recover. Everyone was so happy he'd come out of it okay, that the speech thing...well it was hard on him, but he was alive, you know?"

I wonder if that's why Frank hasn't left Cherry Tree. And if the reason he does so much for the people in town is that he feels indebted for everything they did to help him and his family.

"After he recovered," Evelyn goes on, "Frankie used to run around town with a silver whistle in his mouth making all kinds of noise. Drove everybody up the wall, it did, but he was happy."

I think of the whistle Frank gave to Libby and smile. Evelyn places two cups of tea on the table between us with a *plonk*, then sits, looking at me intently.

"He's grown up to be such a nice young man, hasn't he?"

"Uh, yeah." I'm not sure why, but it feels like there's a purpose to her statement. "I mean, I don't know him very well. But yeah, he seems like a good guy."

"Frankie's such a handsome man, too." She speaks into her cup, not looking at me. "Don't you think?"

"Yeah, he..." I stop myself. There's a prickle of heat creeping up my cheeks. Narrowing my eyes, I ask, "Why?"

"No reason." Evelyn shrugs, eyes full of innocence. "I do wish he'd find someone and get married. I hate thinking about him living all alone in the woods for the rest of his life."

"Maybe he doesn't want to get married. Lots of people choose to live alone."

"You're right. And that's okay," she says. "But I don't think Frankie is one of those people. I don't think he *wants* to be alone forever." Evelyn sips her tea, then raises an eyebrow. "Do you?"

I sigh. "No, probably not. But he's cautious. And for good reason, I think."

"Of course." Evelyn covers my wrist with her own soft, frail hand. "You're his friend. You know Frankie pretty well."

I want to say that no, I don't know Frank that well. But I think maybe I do. Or at least, Frank has revealed more of himself to me than he has to most people around him.

"I guess," I say quietly.

"So you know he has a hard time letting people in."

"Yes, I do." I trace the floral pattern of the tablecloth with the tip of my finger. "I think he wants to be more open. Maybe he just doesn't know how." *God, what must it be like to live your whole adult life with no one to talk to beyond surface level chit chat?*

"These things take time. It's good he has you." There's something in Evelyn's voice that catches my attention, the way she seems to emphasize *he has you*. I nod and stare at my cup, wondering if she's implying what I suspect she is.

Evelyn's kitchen faucet drips and in the back of my mind, I know she'll call Frank to fix it. As we drink our tea, Evelyn asks about Libby, about my job, and about my plans for winter break.

"Is there anything else I can help you with before I go?" I ask, finishing my tea.

"Oh, no sweetheart. But I should thank you for moving that blasted box. You saved me from disturbing Frankie while he's working."

"Frank *would* drop everything to come and help you, wouldn't he?"

"He would," Evelyn says, patting my arm. "He's like a son to me. He's like a son or brother to everyone in this town. I don't think he knows it, but we all want to see him happy."

An unexpected prickle of tears wells in my eyes. She's right—he probably has no idea he has so many people who genuinely care for him.

"And if anyone does anything to hurt him," she says, leveling me with an intense gaze, "there are plenty of people in town to answer to." She grips her cane tightly and raps it on the floor for emphasis.

I set my empty cup down and thank Evelyn for the tea. She walks me to the door, patting me on the back as I leave. Returning to my house, fresh thoughts of Frank swirl through my mind.

The holiday show is exactly as promised: elementary-aged children singing, dancing, and performing skits, all with a non-religious winter theme. There are missed cues, off-key notes, and shy kids who freeze when thrust into the spotlight. But there are some highlights too.

Libby—dressed in sparkly red tights, a white dress, and a headband with a glittery snowflake on top—signs the words to several songs like an ASL interpreter at a music concert. She hadn't told me beforehand, saying it was a surprise. Well, I'm certainly surprised, and impressed. Her ASL skills have improved dramatically since moving here just a few months ago.

She smiles proudly as she signs, trying her best to mouth the words as well. More than a few times, her timing is off, but it doesn't matter. She beams as brightly as the sun, and I know I'm smiling just as brightly.

The only thing that would make this evening perfect is if Frank were here with me—or if he were here at all. Since my call this morning,

I'd kept my phone close, checking often for a reply. Hours had gone by without a response.

When it had been time for Libby to get back to the school for the show, I'd checked one last time for a text from Frank. Finding none, I'd turned off my phone, glumly tucking it away in my coat pocket. I'd known asking him was a longshot anyway.

When the final curtain closes and all the kids are released into the auditorium to find their grownups, chaos ensues. It's not a big school, but still, it's a hundred elementary-aged kids running around, all dressed in costume and buzzing with excitement from being onstage.

At the front of the auditorium, I find Libby and am immediately showered with silver glitter the moment she jumps into my arms. I give her a huge hug, then set her down on her feet and tell her, "I'm so proud of you, my baby girl."

Libby pulls a sour face, just like she does every time I call her that, but I can tell she's pleased.

"Ice cream?" I ask.

She claps, jumping up and down and causing even more glitter to rain into her hair and onto the floor.

"Can Frank come with us?" she asks.

My heart sinks. I don't want to tell her he didn't come, especially when she's so happy right now. But I can't lie to her.

"Frank didn't come," I reply. "I'm sorry."

Libby draws her eyebrows together so tightly that two matching vertical lines appear between them.

"Yes, he did," she says matter-of-factly.

I tilt my head in confusion. "Are you sure?" I ask. "It could've been someone else that—"

"No." She shakes her head. "I saw him over there."

Libby points to a spot near the side door of the auditorium. My heart pounds, hopeful that *maybe* Frank is here. Eyeing the area where she's pointing, I only see a pack of adults I vaguely know gathered in a clump.

"Well, if it was Frank, he's not there now," I tell her, still doubting it actually *was* him. After all, Libby had been on stage with a light on her through most of the show, so it would've been nearly impossible for her to see anything past the first couple rows.

"Let's get some ice cream," I say and sign, then take Libby's hand, making our way past the people lingering to chat. We're a few steps from exiting to the lobby when Libby wrenches her hand out of mine and slips away. I follow, watching her sprint past classmates and adults. My heart bursts with joy when I watch her wrap Frank in an enormous hug.

When I catch up, I take in Frank's appearance. He's wearing old, worn work jeans, a faded red flannel shirt, and a baseball cap pulled low, almost hiding his eyes entirely. His hair and the shoulders of his shirt are flecked with sawdust. His normally short, neatly trimmed beard has gotten a bit longer and more unruly, but it doesn't hide the traces of a smile on his lips.

"Hi, Frank," I say as I approach. "I...I didn't expect to see you here." Despite trying to school my expression, I can't help but smile.

He nods, looking like he might say something more, but Libby jumps in.

"My dad said you wouldn't come because you were too busy," she signs. "But I knew you would." Frank crouches down to Libby's height and she gives him another hug.

"It's great to see you," he signs. "I've missed you."

Frank glances up, catching my eye for a long moment, then looks away. Though he's talking to Libby, I know the comment is meant for me. Butterflies flutter in my chest.

He stands, and we do the awkward dance of *hug or handshake?* I take Frank's hand, leaning in for a hug, and am enveloped by the smell of freshly cut wood and the warmth of his strong arms. When we part, he brushes his fingertips over my chest, dusting away a few bits of sawdust that had rubbed off his shirt and onto mine.

"Sorry. I'm a mess," Frank signs, then switches to texting.

«I was out on calls, then had some work to do in the shop. Saw your message about five minutes before the show started.»

«I didn't get a chance to clean up. Just jumped in the truck and headed over here.»

"Don't apologize," I say. "I'm—we're happy you could come."

Libby tugs on Frank's shirt excitedly. "Did you see me signing all the words?" she asks.

"I did!" Frank replies with exaggerated enthusiasm. "You were great! Would you teach me the words to one of the songs?"

Libby nods eagerly. "I'll teach you *all* the songs!"

Frank gives me a mock "help me" look, but I just laugh.

"I can't help you there," I say to Frank. "You asked for it."

When Frank's eyes linger on me—a little longer than someone who's *just a friend*—a magnetic energy pulls at the space between us. I can't force myself to look away first.

"Frankie?" Evelyn's voice breaks the spell causing us both to snap out of our daze. Frank smiles warmly at Evelyn, who's dressed in rust-colored pants and an olive cardigan. She's wearing a red knitted beanie—just like the one Frank usually wears—over her fluffy white hair.

"Goodness, my boy!" she exclaims, placing her hand on Frank's arm. "What a pleasant surprise to see you here."

Frank nods and gestures toward Libby, then points to the stage.

"You came to see Libby?" she asks, narrowing her eyes. "Well, isn't that nice?"

She looks pointedly at me, a little spark of excitement in her eyes. Frank looks between the two of us with a hint of confusion on his face that I pretend not to notice.

"It's so wonderful to see you come out tonight to support your friends," Evelyn says. "Don't you think?" That question is directed at me.

I clear my throat. "Yes, absolutely," I say. "Being such a familiar face around town, I think Frank probably has lots of friends here tonight."

"Indeed," Evelyn agrees.

"So, are you here to see someone in the show?" I ask her.

"Oh, yes! My great niece. She was the one dressed as a deer."

"Right," I say, vaguely remembering someone with a set of sparkly antlers on the stage. "She was great."

Evelyn beams with pride. Libby tugs on my jacket sleeve and signs "ice cream" in exaggerated motions.

"I should be going before my nephew leaves me behind," Evelyn says. "Good night, Frankie," she says, giving his elbow a squeeze. To me, she just winks, and I think either she knows more about Frank than she's letting on, or...well, I can't think of another reason why she keeps giving me not-so-subtle nudges toward Frank.

We all say our goodbyes to Evelyn, and I help Libby into her coat.

"Come with us for ice cream," Libby signs to Frank.

I fuss with the zipper of Libby's coat, trying not to look up, knowing he'll see the eagerness written on my face.

"I'm sorry," Frank signs. "I can't. Next time, okay?" Libby pouts, but eventually nods. My heart sags with disappointment.

We wade through the lobby and several adults and teachers stop us, complimenting Libby on her performance. A handful of people even stop Frank, greeting him warmly and expressing surprise to see him here. Frank seems equally surprised at the warm reception he receives. It's clear he doesn't attend social events very often. At some point in all the commotion, we get separated and Frank disappears in the crowd. By the time we make it to the exit, I'm convinced he's slipped away quietly and left.

I try not to feel slighted that Frank left without saying goodbye. He was probably overwhelmed by all the people. Pushing the heavy metal door open, a blast of frigid air hits my face and I shiver. Just outside the door, leaning against the brick wall, baseball hat pulled low and jacket zipped all the way up to his chin, is Frank. The smile that crosses his lips is small, almost undetectable, save for the dimple in his cheek that gives him away. The cold suddenly seems insignificant.

Frank pushes off the wall and walks toward me. Libby beams, reaching out and taking his hand, gripping mine with her other hand. The three of us walk toward the parking lot, and I feel lighter than I have all week.

As if by instinct, Frank and I simultaneously raise our arms—the ones holding Libby's hands—swinging her up into the air. She laughs loudly and unselfconsciously.

Last summer, in our old neighborhood in New York, Libby had been at the playground playing tag with a friend. She'd been laughing and shouting excitedly without a care in the world. Two boys a few years older than her had pointed, snickering and loudly asking why she sounded weird. She'd been wearing her hearing aids, and though she hadn't heard the boys' exact words, she knew they were being unkind about the way she sounded. While I tried my best to smooth things over for her, the incident had made Libby self-conscious of her voice, and she's rarely used it since.

But now, she laughs loudly without a second thought, and my heart nearly bursts from the sheer joy of the sounds she makes.

Once...twice...three times...we lift Libby by the arms and swing her, feet kicking higher each time. I venture a glance at Frank who's grinning almost as widely and unabashedly as Libby. Our gazes catch for just a moment and I almost can't breathe.

My heart breaks, just a little, at the idea that Frank doesn't want more than this—more than friendship. *But maybe he does.* Maybe I just need to wait.

CHAPTER 11

FRANK

I curse myself the entire drive home from the holiday show. Why does this perfect man and his perfect daughter have to be so...so fucking *perfect*? I thought if I told myself I was fine being alone—after all, I've been alone for my entire adult life—then I'd get over these feelings I have for Bennett.

Problem is, Cherry Tree is a small town. There's no way to avoid seeing Bennett at least once a week, especially when I'm out and about doing my handyman work.

Problem is, Bennett is trying to fix up his house on his own and doesn't know much about, well, about fixing up a house. He needs my help.

Problem is, Bennett is the only person who's truly ever bothered to really get to know me. He asks questions and listens thoughtfully to my answers. He's patient as I muddle through signing, and patient while I type my answers on the phone.

Problem is, Bennett's the best person I know. He's smart—much smarter than me. He went to college and got his Ph.D. for god's sake. He's handsome and sophisticated, beautiful.

And what do I have to offer? I'm average looking at best—not bad to look at, muscular, but a little softer than I'd like. I don't have a college degree. I don't have a fancy job nurturing the brilliant young minds of a younger generation.

No, I'm a college dropout. A handyman who's mostly paid in sandwiches and desserts. Okay, well, that's only my side job, but still... I work alone in my workshop and only have my dogs to keep me company. *And I can't fucking speak.*

By the time I return home, I've let my thoughts spiral to the point I'm thoroughly convinced I'd done the right thing by pushing Bennett away. I've had three decades to build this wall around myself, practically guaranteeing no one can hurt me, and shutting out nearly everyone around me in the process.

Realization dawns that this line of thinking is likely the result of going to bed well after midnight every night and waking up before sunrise every morning for the last two weeks. I'm drained, both physically and mentally. The holiday season always does this to me. By Christmas, I'm so exhausted, I have no interest in being festive, politely declining invitations from various townsfolk—they're most likely out of pity anyway. It's one of the reasons I don't put up a tree or lights. It always feels like I'm looking through a window as other people—people with loved ones—celebrate the holidays.

I really need to get back to the workshop and finish the end tables I'd been working on, which thankfully hadn't been ordered in time for Christmas. But after seeing Bennett, followed by my mental spiral, I have no energy left. I let the dogs out one final time for the night, stoke the fire, then lay on the couch. I turn on the television, then turn it back off again. I check my phone, hoping for a message from Bennett, but find no texts waiting for me. For a moment, I think about texting him, but I have no idea what I'd even say, so I don't. It's just as well. I shower, then go to bed.

Wednesday morning, I wake to a few inches of snow outside and a few requests for last-minute holiday help. Big Jim—ironically named since he's barely 5'4" and skinny as a rail—hit an ice patch last night, sending his car off the road into a ditch. He'd walked home, but needed help pulling his car out. Barry, the owner of the only bar in town, has a burst pipe that's leaking into the basement and no plumbers are available. Marybeth bought her fiancé a flat-screen television, but needs help mounting it to the wall to surprise him. And on and on it goes all morning.

It's well past lunchtime before I'm able to check on the Walkers' vacation house. I'd gotten an alert that there had been activity that tripped the motion detector in front of the house. It's likely a deer, as it almost always is, and since Wednesday is one of my usual days for checking on the house, I head there before I'm called away by someone else in need of help.

The driveway is already occupied by another car that I instantly recognize as belonging to Jules. I scan my recent texts to see if I've missed a message from Jules letting me know he'll be coming, but there's nothing. I'm surprised he's here considering he was just here with his friends a month ago for Thanksgiving weekend.

I sit in the truck—melting snow falling from the trees like rain onto the windshield—wondering whether I should knock on the door, or turn around and go. Jules hadn't messaged me, so maybe he doesn't want me to know he's here.

Thankfully, the front door opens, and his smiling face appears, radiating warmth. I feel a rush of affection seeing Jules in person for the first time in more than a year.

He's wearing a white cashmere sweater that perfectly complements his dark skin and black hair, a black, flowy maxi skirt, and white high-top sneakers with tall, chunky heels. Stepping onto the porch, he waves, gesturing for me to come to the door.

"Frank!" he exclaims, hugging me tightly the moment I'm in front of him. I can't help but smile. I don't see Jules often, but he always greets me like a close friend.

«You should've told me you were coming. I would've gotten the house ready for you. There's no food.»

"It was a spur of the moment thing," Jules says. "My friends and I needed to get out of town for a little while."

«I'll go to the store and pick up some things for you.»

"Oh, no," he says, waving me off. "You don't need to do that. I can go to the store later."

«No.»

I emphasize my text with a vigorous shake of my head.

«Taking care of the house and preparing it for your visits is what your parents pay me to do.»

«Besides, you're probably tired from the long drive.»

Jules sighs. "My parents don't pay you to stock the fridge for me and my friends, but fine. *Only* because I've never seen you argue. Like *ever*. And you're right. We're all pretty tired."

«I'll get the usual things, and some stuff to make a couple of easy meals.»

"You're a lifesaver, you know that?"

«Does anyone need toiletries? Toothpaste, shampoo, anything like that?»

"I think we have all that here from when we came at Thanksgiving."

«Text me if you think of anything else. I'll be back soon.»

An hour later, I pull into the driveway for the second time today, this time with groceries in the back of my truck. I unload the bags, carrying several at once. Jules opens the door, taking a couple of the bags from my hands, and following me inside.

Normally, I'd leave everything with Jules, say goodbye, and go home. But I don't want to leave. Bennett must've really gotten into my head, because I find myself wanting to be around people...for no other reason than for the company.

I line up the bags on the counter and begin to unpack them.

"Don't worry about that," Jules says. "I'll put everything away."

I shake my head and continue until everything is in its place. When I run out of things to do, I turn to leave. Remembering one last purchase I'd made in town, I message Jules that I'll be right back. I jog to the truck, returning a moment later with a box of fresh pastries. Handing it to him, I suddenly feel awkward, like this is stepping over some invisible boundary of employer-employee.

I tell myself I need to be open to making more friends, so I'm going to try. Jules has always been so kind to me and seems like he wants to be my friend. Only, I don't really know *how* to do this.

Apparently oblivious to my internal crisis, Jules squeals with joy when he opens the pastry box.

"Oh. My. God," he says, punctuating each word. "You're a superhero!"

My cheeks flush, and I laugh to myself. *Superhero.*

Jules calls for his friends to come to the kitchen.

"Frank," Bastián, Jules' oldest friend and roommate says, stepping in the kitchen. "¡Cuánto tiempo sin verte!"

Indeed, it's been years since I'd seen him. So many, in fact, that the awkward preteen has grown into a young man. Bastián wraps me in a hug.

"¿Estás bien?"

I nod, feeling touched that he'd remembered me.

A second young man, a little younger than Bastián, watches us from the shadows of the hall. He's wearing a hoodie that obscures most of his face, and he has a blanket wrapped tightly around his shoulders.

"That's Gael," Jules says, raising his chin in the young man's direction. "He's Bastián's boyfriend."

I wave at the stranger.

"Frank's my friend," Jules explains. "I've known him almost my whole life."

The acknowledgement that Jules regards me as a friend fills me with gratitude. I feel a little silly knowing he doesn't grasp how much it means to me that he's said it.

I pick up the box of pastries and hold it out to Gael who takes one cautiously.

"Thank you," he says quietly.

"You're welcome," I sign. I'm not sure Gael can read sign language, but understanding crosses his face. He gives me a small, almost imperceptible smile before hurrying back down the hall and disappearing into the bedroom.

I should go, I know I should. I have a long list of things I need to do at home.

"Frank?" Jules says. "You okay?"

Nodding quickly, I pull my phone out and text him before I can second guess myself.

«Can I talk to you about something? It's kind of personal.»

"Of course," he says. He ushers us both into the living room. Bastián takes another pastry from the box, waves goodbye, and disappears down the hall, leaving us alone.

"What's up?" Jules asks, settling onto the couch. I sit on the opposite end, my leg bouncing rapidly.

Now that I have his attention, I don't know how to talk about this. I'm not even sure what I want to know. All I know is that I need to talk.

I type on my phone, delete, then type again. Over and over, I start, stop, then start again. Jules waits patiently, but I'm struggling.

"Frank, love," he says, scooting closer and putting a hand on my arm. "It's okay."

Looking into Jules' concerned eyes, I nod, then finally type a message and send it before I can delete it again.

«Do you think I'm good looking?»

Jules cocks his head to the side, clearly not expecting the question. But he doesn't laugh, thank god.

"Of course I do," he says, like it's the most obvious answer. "I believe I've told you at least half a dozen times that if I were ten years older and single, I'd be into you."

I dip my head in embarrassment.

"But, you know I'm with Evie, right?" he asks slowly.

I wave my hands and emphatically shake my head *no*.

«That's not why I was asking. Sorry.»

"I'm just teasing you," he chuckles. Then his face turns serious. "Why are you asking, though?"

I bite my lip and stare at my phone. *I can talk to him about this. Jules is a friend.*

«I like someone.»

"Oh?" Jules raises his perfectly groomed eyebrows. "Do they know?"

«Yes.»

«Well, kind of.»

"Okay, you're going to have to tell me more." He leans forward, resting his elbows on his knees.

«We kissed.»

"Yesssss, Frank!" Jules beams, giving my shoulder a playful shove. "So, they like you, too?"

«Yeah. But then I said we should just be friends.»

"Why?"

This is the part I've been dreading. Because I know that telling another person my reasons is going to sound ridiculous. But I can't back out now. With a sigh, I type.

«He's smart. College professor smart.»

"Wait. He's *as smart as* a college professor, or he *is* a college professor?"

I hold up two fingers indicating the second answer.

«He teaches English.»

I wait for Jules to comment on—or at least raise an eyebrow at—the fact that the person I like is a man, but to my relief, he doesn't react to that part at all.

"Okay, go on."

«He's traveled a lot. He moved here from New York.»

«He's really good looking. Beautiful.»

«He's kind. He's patient with me when we talk. He's interested in what I have to say.»

"Still not understanding why you said you wanted to just be friends with him."

«Because he's perfect.»

«And I'm me.»

Jules throws his head back, groaning dramatically. My face fills with heat and I stare down at my phone to avoid his look of dismay.

"First of all," he says, sitting up straighter, "*you* are smart. You may not have a fancy degree in English literature or whatever, but I've known you a long time. You read a lot. You write texts in complete sentences." I snort, but Jules goes on. "You know so much about so many things. You know how to scare bears away. You can fix anything. You literally built your own house, for god's sake! Do you know how many people *can't* do any of those things? A lot, myself included."

I chuckle.

«Being able to scare a bear and being able to talk intelligently about literature are two very different things.»

"Exactly," he says. "I'd like to see Mister Perfect scare a bear away by reciting Shakespeare at it."

I laugh again, harder this time, allowing my voice to be heard.

"Why on earth are you comparing yourself to this guy? There are different ways to be smart."

«I don't know. I guess I'm just feeling a little bit like I'm not enough.»

«Not good enough, I guess?»

"Not good enough? Frank!" His tone is incredulous. "You're kind. You do so much for the community, most of it for free. You build furniture with your hands. You take in stray dogs. You're thoughtful. You bring my favorite treats when you know I'm coming, even though I know you have to go all the way to Traverse City to get them."

I stare at Jules, though I want nothing more than to look away.

"You're good enough." He jabs a finger into the meat of my bicep. "You're better than good enough...and I think you know it."

I pick at a loose thread in my shirt, averting my eyes from his razor-sharp stare. He folds his arms and leans against the back of the couch, not saying anything while I squirm under his shrewd gaze.

"You want to know what I think?" he finally asks. When I shrug, he goes on. "I think you're using the *I'm not good enough* line as an excuse for something else. It's too easy. So, what is it *really*?"

My shoulders sag and I sink into the couch. Taking a deep breath, I stare at my phone, tapping on the edge as I think about how to respond. If I'm going to try to open myself up to other potential friendships—and if I want to get real advice on what I should do about Bennett—I need to be honest.

«You're right.»

«I mean, it's true, I do feel all those things I said. But to be honest, it's not the biggest reason for pushing him away.»

Jules' eyes flick from his phone to my face and back again as he waits for more.

«I've been alone my whole life. As a kid, I was sick or in the hospital so much. I was gone for almost a whole year. And then after my surgery, I struggled to keep friends.»

«I've had acquaintances, surface level friends. I even tried having a girlfriend once, for two weeks in high school. But most people never really knew me. Partly because communicating with me takes time and patience that a lot of people don't have.»

«But also because I don't let people get to know me.»

"Why not?" His tone is much softer now.

I sigh, looking at the ceiling for a moment before typing.

«When you spend a lifetime being talked at, talked over, or not being talked to at all, eventually you believe you have nothing worth saying.»

Jules reads the message, then glances at me with sad, glistening eyes. I look back down, subtly wiping my eyes with my sleeve and hoping he doesn't notice.

«I learned to build walls to protect myself from getting hurt. I don't let myself get too close to other people. I tried having friends when I was younger. But they would get frustrated by my disability and decide I wasn't worth the effort. They'd gradually fade away, until one day, they weren't part of my life anymore. It happened a lot.»

«It was never malicious, and I don't think anyone knew how much it hurt. But it did.»

«So I stopped letting it happen.»

It's the first time I've ever talked about this with anyone. If I'm being honest, it's something I try hard to not even think about. I hate self-pity, and I've been doing a lot of it lately. I thought talking about this with Jules would be difficult or exposing. But deep down, I knew he was the right person to confide in. From what I know about him, Jules had a rough time growing up too, being Black and queer in a predominantly white suburb of Chicago. I think maybe he can relate, at least a little bit.

After a long moment, Jules says, "So, this guy...?"

«Bennett. He's the first person I've let in since... I don't know when. We've become really good friends. I'm scared that if things don't work out, I'll lose him as a friend too.»

«I know it sounds silly that I care so much about losing one friend, but he's the only friend I have, and losing him would hurt so much more.»

«I don't want to go back to being completely alone. Even if it's not a romantic relationship, I want to keep him.»

"I get that," Jules says. "A really good friend can be like a soul mate."

I nod, swallowing the lump that's formed in my throat.

"How's it been since you told him you just wanted to be friends?"

«Honestly? A little weird. We're kind of awkward around each other. I've been kind of avoiding him since that happened.»

"I see." He narrows his eyes.

«If it weren't for his daughter, I probably wouldn't have seen him at all.»

"He's a dad?"

«Yeah, that's another thing I'm kind of worried about. She loves me. What happens if things don't work out? I don't want to upset or disappoint her.»

"Good lord!" Jules throws his hands in the air and stands before collecting himself and sitting back down.

«What?»

"You're coming up with every excuse you can think of to tell yourself you shouldn't be with this guy. Yet, you still like him, and you're asking my advice about what to do about him. Why?"

Maybe this wasn't such a good idea after all. Jules is cutting straight to the heart of my feelings, and I'm not sure I want him to see my insecurities laid bare in front of him like this. But no. I want advice, and I'll never get it by avoiding the truth.

«Because he's incredible. I'm so happy when I'm around him. I can totally be myself. I feel seen by him. I've never had anyone who could make me feel like that.»

Jules gives me the most wicked smile. I make a *what?* gesture.

"You're in love with him."

He says it so simply, like it's not a question at all. And, really, it isn't. I *am* in love with Bennett. *How had that happened?* I put my head in my hands, raking my fingers through my hair before sitting up and typing again.

«I guess I am.»

«What should I do?»

"You need to talk to him. Tell him this 'just friends' arrangement is poppycock. Tell him all the things you told me."

«I can't tell him all of that. He'll run away for sure.»

"Babe, he won't. If this guy is as great as you say he is, then you owe it to him to be honest. It doesn't mean you have to jump into a relationship right away, or confess your love to him. But you need to talk to him."

«I know.»

"Trust me," he says, putting a hand on my arm. "You'll both feel better."

I furrow my brow, staring at the floor. I know he's right. Bennett is understanding. He's patient. He'd get it. Finally, I nod.

"You will?"

I nod more resolutely this time.

"Do you promise?"

«Yes, I promise.»

Jules watches me expectantly.

«Not right this minute.»

"Why not?"

«Because I need some time to think about what to say. And I need a shower.»

"Okay, fine. But soon, right?"

«Yes.»

After our chat, I feel lighter. But I'm not ready to face Bennett just yet.

I talk Jules into letting me cook dinner for him and his friends since they've spent the last several hours on the road. It's not anything fancy: spaghetti with jarred sauce that I jazz up with some vegetables and herbs, toasted bread with garlic butter, and a homemade cherry pie I'd made and frozen over the summer. I pop the pie into the oven to warm up as I cook the rest of the meal.

The four of us eat dinner at the large oak dining table that my dad and I made together for Jules' parents years ago. Afterwards, Gael helps me wash the dishes, and we work in easy silence while Jules and Bastián talk animatedly, laughing and joking in the living room.

Remembering I need to go home to let the dogs out, I say goodbye to Bastián and Gael, promising I'll visit the next time they come to town. Jules walks me to my truck, pestering me to call Bennett the whole time.

I promise half a dozen times that I will, and that I'll give Jules a full report when I do. Before I leave, I text:

«Thank you for listening. I'm sorry it took so long for me to realize you were my friend all along.»

"You know," he says. "You have more people around you that could be your friend...if you'd let them in." My throat tightens and I blink away tears.

«I know. I'm going to try.»

«I promise.»

Jules hugs me and gives a kiss on the cheek before going back inside. I sit in the driveway for a minute, smiling to myself thinking about the past two hours. *Friends.*

Waking just before seven o'clock, I toss and turn, trying to go back to sleep. Thoughts of my conversation with Jules fill my head. My stomach is a ball of nerves, but I know I'll feel worse if I stay in bed.

I'm filled with equal parts dread and excitement as I try to imagine the conversation I ~~want~~ need to have with Bennett. It's too early to do anything about it now, so instead, I pull on a pair of sweatpants, a jacket, and hiking boots and head outside with the dogs.

The sun isn't due to rise for another hour, but ribbons of pale pink are beginning to streak over the horizon. A chilly mist shrouds the trees and dances over the glassy surface of the lake. The scents of dry leaves and moss hang heavy in the air, and puffs of white fog cloud my face with every breath. My boots squelch along the muddy trail that snakes in and out of the trees and follows the edge of the lake. As I walk, I take in huge lungfuls of air, trying to center myself. The caws of a few stubborn crows that haven't migrated for the winter break the silence.

The lake hasn't frozen over yet, so I make sure the dogs don't wander onto the thin ice. When they get too close to the edge of the water, I blow my whistle in two quick chirps, and they immediately come back.

After a while, the sun crests the horizon, sending beams of orange light across the surface of the lake. Unsure how long I've been outside, I whistle for the dogs, and they lead the way back to the house. Once inside, I clean the mud off their paws, then take a long, hot shower.

My phone is quiet so far, and I take that as a sign that it's a good day to talk to Bennett. I drink my coffee, forcing myself to take long, slow sips. *Take it easy.* Glancing at the clock, it's just after nine—not so early that I'd wake Bennett.

I brush my teeth and tug on my boots. As I'm about to go, my eyes catch on the gift I'd been making for Libby. I finished it last night, wrapping it and setting it on the counter, waiting for the next time I see her. I snatch it off the table, give Boo and Butter a few ear scratches, then head out. As I drive, excitement and dread ebb and flow, each one swelling and receding like ocean waves. I've had all night and all morning to think about how to approach the conversation, and still, I don't know.

Turning onto Main Street, Cherry Tree looks like a ghost town. Shops that should be open are closed, and there isn't a soul to be seen on the sidewalk. Giant tinsel snowflakes are strung over the streets, and oversized candy canes hang from streetlights, but there's no one on the roads or sidewalks to enjoy them.

Realization dawns. It's Christmas. *How had I not remembered?* With all of the work I'd been doing in the shop and helping people around town, I'd somehow lost track of the days.

I round the corner and idle at the stop sign a block from Bennett's house. No one else is on the road, so I sit at the intersection, trying to work out what to do. My truck rumbles as I contemplate whether I should keep going toward Bennett's house, or go home and come back tomorrow.

Thinking I should let Bennett and Libby enjoy their holiday, I crank the steering wheel to make a U-turn when my phone buzzes with a call. I huff a sigh, hoping it isn't someone with a burst pipe or overflowing toilet that needs fixing as I fish the phone out of my pocket. My heart hammers when I read the name of the caller: Bennett.

Swiping to accept the call, I pull over and press the phone to my ear.

"Frank? Hi, it's Bennett. You probably knew that. Uh, Merry Christmas. I'm calling because I have an emergency and I was wondering if you could help me. Of course, if you have your own plans, it can wait. You probably already have plans. I can call back tomorrow if—"

I shake my head, smiling. I type out a message while Bennett's still talking.

«What's the emergency?»

"Oh, right. Well, my heat stopped working. The furnace made a terrible clanking sound and now it's not doing anything..."

I switch the phone to speaker, then pull my truck away from the curb, turning toward Bennett's house.

"And, the lights started flickering all over the house. And the toilet's overflowing and getting water all over. Um, and I think there's a raccoon family in the attic. I can hear them having one big rodent party up there. And the roof is leaking and there's rain coming in..."

I glance up at the sky: clear, definitely *not* raining.

"And there's a possum under the front porch that keeps biting Libby's ankles every time she walks by. And…"

I laugh, scratchy and low. Bennett must hear because he finally stops talking.

«And?»

"And…" Bennett pauses and I think I might have lost connection. "And I miss you. I was hoping you could come over—if you don't have other plans, of course. Even if it's just as friends, I want you to spend Christmas with us. With…me."

I park my truck in front of the house, and jog up the steps to the porch. My heart is racing, and I can't keep from smiling.

I take one steadying breath, then knock on the door.

CHAPTER 12

BENNETT

"Hang on," I say into the phone. "Someone's knocking on the door."

I'm already showered and dressed, wearing a pair of dark jeans and a cream-colored sweater despite knowing this color is a risk with a small child in the house. I put it on because it brings out my eyes—or so the salesperson had said when I tried it on—and I want to look good in case Frank comes over today.

I'd been thinking about making this phone call since the day Frank showed up at Libby's holiday show. There's been so much awkward air between us since he put the brakes on after we kissed, but I know the desire for more is still there. I vowed I wouldn't push him, but I want to make it clear that I'm open for whatever he's ready for. If Frank comes over and all we do is hang out, I'd be okay with that. I miss Frank and want to be with him in whatever way he wants. And most importantly, I want him to know that we're friends, and that he's welcome here, he's wanted.

I pad across the entryway in my wool socks with the phone still pressed to my ear.

"It's probably Evelyn coming to bring us a fruitcake," I say. "She's been threatening, I mean promising, to bring one. Don't tell her I said that."

When I pull the door open, I freeze, nearly dropping the phone. Frank is standing on the porch dressed in a chunky, navy blue sweater and his worn black coat. He's wearing a striped scarf that looks like the one Evelyn had been furiously knitting the last two weeks. A huge smile splits across my face.

"Frank?" My voice sounds breathless. "How did you...?" My mind is too jumbled to finish my sentence. I shake my head, as if to knock my thoughts loose again. "How did you get here so fast?"

"I was already on my way over," Frank signs, stepping closer.

"Why?" I immediately want to kick myself.

"Because I don't want to be friends with you." My pulse skids to a halt. "You...don't?"

Frank shakes his head. "I want more. If you do."

I'm flooded with happiness, and my heart nearly bursts. I step forward, closing the gap between us.

"I still want it," I whisper, my lips brushing Frank's brows. "I still want you."

He reaches out, clutching a handful of my sweater, pulling until there's almost no space between us. I tip his chin up with my knuckle, then lean down, brushing a light kiss to the corner of his mouth. He lets out a gravelly moan, and I slide a hand around the back of his head, pulling his face closer.

I let my tongue glide lightly along Frank's bottom lip, tasting toothpaste and the faintest hint of coffee. He responds by parting his lips slightly and relaxing, letting himself lean into me. This time, I'm the one who moans, covering his mouth with my own and kissing him deeply.

"My word!" a voice calls from inside the house. "Who's letting all the cold air in?"

Frank and I break our kiss, but remain close, my arm around his waist. From the hallway, my mom, Cheryl, appears with a festive red cardigan wrapped tightly around her shoulders.

"Frankie Garza!" she exclaims. "Well, it's been forever and a day since I've seen you! Merry Christmas!" She pushes past me to give Frank a hug, then steps back, looking him up and down.

Frank nods, signing *hello* and fingerspelling her name.

"My, my. I'm so happy to see you again. You're looking good." She smiles at Frank, then gives me a little wink. I resist the urge to roll my eyes. "When I heard the knock on the door, I thought it was Evelyn bringing that dreadful fruit cake over."

"Mom!" I scold. "Be nice."

"Oh, psshh." Mom waves a hand dismissively. "She's a lovely lady. But her fruit cake isn't winning any awards."

I shake my head, chuckling. "It's not that bad. Frank, back me up. Have you ever eaten Evelyn's fruit cake?"

"Allergic," he signs.

"You're not missing out," Mom says with a wry smile.

"Mom, would you mind giving us a minute?" She looks between us. "We were...talking."

"Oh! Sure, son." Her eyes twinkle and she grins. "But at least come inside out of the cold. Poor Frankie's going to freeze out here."

"Just Frankie?" I ask. Frank glares at my use of his childhood nickname.

"You'll be fine," Mom says, brushing me off. "Come on now." She pulls Frank by the sleeve and shuts the door behind us. "I'll go play with Libby. Take all the time you need."

But before she leaves, Libby's footsteps echo in the hall. Catching sight of Frank, she bursts out in a sprint and jumps into his arms excitedly. She hugs him tightly and buries her face in his neck.

"Libby certainly likes you," Mom remarks, smiling. Frank lets Libby slide down until her feet hit the floor. He kneels and signs, "Merry Christmas."

"I knew you would come today," she signs back. "Daddy thought you wouldn't come, but I knew you would."

"I had to," Frank says. "I needed to give you this." He pulls something small out of his pocket that's wrapped in red fabric and tied with a simple white ribbon.

Libby takes it, turning it over in her hands. She looks at Frank, then up at me. I shrug.

"Open it," Frank signs.

Libby pulls the ribbon and unfolds the red fabric, revealing two tiny wooden dogs, hand carved and painted to look like Boo and Butter. Inspecting each one closely, Libby holds them up for me to see.

"Did you make these?" I ask, already knowing the answer.

"Yes," Frank says.

"They're beautiful, Frank. Thank you for making them for her." He ducks his head, and I detect a blush on his cheeks.

"Well, what a lovely gift," Mom says, doing her best to sign the words to Libby as well. She's still learning to read and sign in ASL. "Let's thank Frank, and go find a nice place to put them in your room. Then we'll make some Christmas cookies."

Libby hugs Frank, then holds both pieces in one hand while she signs *thank you* with the other before Mom steers her toward the stairs.

"Frank," Mom calls. He looks up at her. "You'll stay here a while, right?"

He nods.

"Good," she says. "See you boys in a bit." She winks, then follows Libby up the stairs. I let out a relieved breath, then laugh.

"My mom," I say, still chuckling. "She's—"

But I don't get to finish my sentence. Frank cups my face and pulls me close, kissing me with such determination, I nearly fall backward.

Once I regain my balance, I walk Frank back until he's against the door. Frank smiles under my lips.

"What's so funny?" I ask between kisses.

"D-E-J-A V-U," he fingerspells.

"Ah." I smile. I kiss his ear and whisper, "I really hope things end better than they did that night."

Frank nods and I let myself be kissed again. A few more minutes and many kisses later, I follow as he takes me by the hand and leads me into the living room where a short, wide tree stands, fully decorated with colored lights and an eclectic mix of ornaments. A mess of torn wrapping paper and toys in boxes surrounds the tree, the result of a six o'clock gift-opening frenzy. We sit on the couch, facing each other.

"So," I say, intertwining my fingers with Frank's. "Did something happen that made you change your mind?"

Frank reluctantly pulls his hand from mine and signs, "I talked to a friend."

"A friend?" I ask, raising an eyebrow. "So you *do* have more friends."

I watch as he looks down at the floor for a moment.

"I do. I'm trying." He shakes his head.

"I understand what you mean." I take his hand and kiss his knuckles.

Frank leans back, tipping his head to rest on my shoulder. He slides his phone out of his pocket and types on the notepad app with his free hand, turning it to show me.

«I have some things I need to talk to you about.»

"Okaaaay," I say cautiously.

«It's nothing bad, just some things about me that'll help you to understand why I got scared.»

"I'd like to know whenever you're ready to tell me."

«I will. But maybe one more kiss first?»

I laugh. "I like the sound of that."

Frank sets his phone on the coffee table and scoots closer to me. Pulling him in, I kiss him soundly, wanting him to know I'm here for him. That I'll always be here for him.

"Can you stay for the day?"

Frank shakes his head. "Dogs," he signs.

"Go get them," I whisper into his neck as I inhale, filling my lungs with the scent of Frank: peppermint soap and sawdust, and the faint smell of woodsmoke. "Bring them over so you can stay. Please."

"What about your family?" he asks.

"I want to spend Christmas with my family," I say. "Hot chocolate, and cookies, and board games, and...you."

I kiss Frank's neck, his jaw, the tender spot between his collarbones, causing him to shudder. When I look up at his face, I can see the telltale sparkle in his eyes—fresh tears waiting to fall. I sit up, cupping his face in my hands and staring into his rich, chocolate-brown eyes.

"Frank, I really like you. You know that, right?" He doesn't answer, just stares at me, as if in wonder.

When I woke up this morning, I hadn't thought I'd be putting my heart on the line for Frank, and before I've had breakfast, no less. But here I am. And here's Frank in front of me, staring like I'm speaking a whole other language. Maybe I *am* speaking another language—one that includes him as more than an afterthought, more than a quiet presence in the background of other peoples' lives.

If this kind of talk is foreign to Frank, then I'll gladly spend my life teaching him. I want everything for him. But most of all, I want him to know he's seen, he's heard, and he's loved.

"I like you, too," Frank signs. "So much." He smiles warmly at me, those kind eyes looking at me so tenderly.

"Merry Christmas," I whisper into his ear.

Frank's eyes flutter closed for a moment, a single tear escaping down his cheek. I swipe it away with the sleeve of my sweater. He takes my hand, kisses it, and places it over his chest.

Under my palm, Frank's heartbeat is strong and fast. He points to his heart, then to me. It doesn't take me long to interpret the meaning. *Because of you.* He might not be able to speak words out loud, but he has so much to say, and it fills my heart with joy that he's willing to tell me.

Maybe I don't need to teach Frank my language. Maybe we'll learn from each other and build our own language of love. Together.

ACKNOWLEDGEMENTS

The main character, Frank, was inspired quite a lot by my dad. Despite being "retired" and in his 70s, I still find him climbing a ladder to patch someone's roof, crawling into an attic to fix a faulty electrical system, or digging under a house to repair bad plumbing. He's always been the kind of person everyone knows they can call when they need help. When he's not doing that, he's building in his woodshop or making things to sell on the weekends. So, thanks Dad, for always being there for me and for everyone around you.

Huge thanks, as always, to Peter Senftleben. Your kind words, encouragement, expertise, and tough love continue to make me a better writer. Thank you, Jackson Hollingsworth for your thoughtful insight, both as a sensitivity reader and with line edits. Your clear, thoughtful explanations not only helped me to make this book better, but will continue to be a guide on future projects.

Thank you to Jay Leigh for coming up with the idea for the Home for the Holidays collection and for working so put this all together. Thanks to Dallas Smith for inviting me to join and for doing all the heavy lifting of formatting the entire series. And to the whole group of authors from the Home for the Holidays series for being so kind and welcoming! I appreciate you all!

And the biggest thanks to you, readers, for giving my characters the chance to be heard! I especially wanted to write this for all the introverts, the houseplants. As a fellow houseplant, I truly enjoyed writing this book and giving a voice to someone who felt their words weren't worth being listened to. I see you and I hear you.